CW00530849

THE SLUM LADY

Emma Hardwick

COPYRIGHT

Title: The Slum Lady

Paperback published in 2021

ISBN: 9798745129469

BOOK CARD

Other books by Emma Hardwick

The Urchin of Walton Hall

Forging the Shilling Girl

The Sailor's Lost Daughters

The Scullery Maid's Salvation

The Widow of the Valley

The Christmas Songbird

The Vicar's Wife

The Lost Girl's Beacon of Hope

CONTENTS

1

THE PARTY AT THE ESTATE

Sir Rufus Hamilton-Gordon's transport was fit for royalty. The polished black cab shone like a mirror. The carriage, adorned with understated carvings and gilded filigree-work, displayed the family crest discreetly. The wheels rumbled past the gates of the Leicesters' country estate at precisely three o'clock on a Thursday afternoon. It was the last in an array of arrivals for a weekend-long birthday celebration.

"You are going to adore Dianna," enthused Elizabeth to her brother as she spotted the arrival. "She is the same age as me, twenty-one. We were at school together."

"Far too young," replied Daniel dismissively.

"Oh, Daniel! She is very clever—and she is beautiful. Every young man wants to marry her. You need to act before she is taken by somebody else."

"I am a grown-up, I don't need a matchmaker Elizabeth," he sighed, "I am old enough to find a woman by myself, and it would not be a twenty-one-year-old."

"But you are taking so long, Daniel, and you are already thirty-five, it is time to settle and have a family."

"I cannot believe I am getting a lecture from you, Elizabeth," he said irritated by his youngest sibling's precocious and opinionated attitude. "I have a career that I love, and I am not going to swap it for a woman just yet!"

Elizabeth rolled her eyes petulantly.

"You cannot run around the world digging in old ruins forever. Get a permanent university post and set up a home. Publish more of those books that have made you famous, I am sure that you can do that and have a family."

"You sound like your mother, Elizabeth, and it does not become you. Go away and do whatever young girls do on their birthdays but leave me alone. I hope that you won't marry the first man that you see—because you can."

"It is 1895, Daniel, and I am a modern woman now. I am entitled to have an opinion." Elizabeth put her nose in the air as she admonished him.

The more Elizabeth spoke, the more it annoyed Daniel. Eventually, he ignored her having had enough of her conversation. He settled into a deep leather chair, picked up a book and began to read. She realised that she would not get any more out of Daniel, and she left the room with a flourish that he ignored. Soon, Daniel was absorbed in the ancient civilizations of the Middle East, which was more entertaining than the weekend activities promised to be.

Daniel Leicester disliked Sir Rufus Hamilton-Gordon the instant that he emerged from the carriage. He knew that it was terrible to judge people at first sight, but his instincts seldom failed him.

The city gent was dressed immaculately, which gave the impression that he had set out to impress the family. Sir Rufus had a gaunt face with a sallow complexion. His head was completely bald, yet he had a lush white beard which was trimmed perfectly. He had a nervous energy about him, always a sign of a man set on making an impression.

The gentleman climbed out of the cab with an eager dexterity. He moved like a puppet on a string. His movements were jerky, and he lifted his skinny little knees higher than he needed to. He did not assist his daughter out of the carriage. Instead, he strode directly to his hosts, with his hand stretched out ahead of him, leaving the footman to help Dianna disembark.

If Dianna was embarrassed by her father's behaviour, she did not show it. She was slight like Sir Rufus and looked more like a sixteen-year-old than the twenty-one-year-old that Elizabeth claimed she was. In her snow-white dress, Dianna seemed little more than a girl, and the man in Daniel watched the virtuous young woman being led up the steps to the house. Elizabeth was correct. Dianna was beautiful, but she was aware of it. Dianna's eyes darted from side to side, trying to ascertain who was watching her. At the same time, her over-enthusiastic father danced at her side. Sir Rufus was delighted to introduce her to the Leicesters but spent a tad too long introducing her to Daniel.

"My daughter, my treasure," Sir Rufus crooned.

"I am pleased to meet you," Daniel said with a polite smile.

"Dianna is delighted to meet you," Rufus stated on her behalf.

"Yes, I see," Daniel replied.

"Perhaps, you will help her settle in?"

Sir Rufus was embarrassing the younger man.

"Perhaps," answered Daniel gazing into the distance.

Sir Rufus realised that he was being given a cue to move on. Thankfully, the man was astute and hurried along the reception line.

Dianna was whisked away by Elizabeth and Daniel could not miss that Rufus Hamilton-Gordon had arrived with an agenda, probably to find a suitor for his daughter. Daniel compared Dianna to a lamb being led to the slaughter.

Daniel turned around and made for his father's study to find a quiet spot to have a drink without being disturbed. Sir James Leicester was sitting behind his desk, and before Daniel could escape, his father summoned him into the room. Daniel poured himself a whisky and watched the older man over the rim of his glass.

Sir James cleared his throat, a tell-tale nervous tick always displayed before he began a serious conversation.

"A marriage between you and Dianna will be a political match made in heaven, Daniel," said his father, followed by a smug smile as he puffed on a fat cigar. "It is a fact, the Hamilton-Gordon estate is virtually bankrupt, but Rufus is from old money which opens a lot of powerful doors for our family."

Daniel and his father had an antagonistic relationship, and Sir Leicester often wondered where he had gone wrong raising his son. Daniel had no political ambitions, no respect for the aristocracy, and on many occasions, James had to lecture him on his etiquette in the company of the elite. Daniel was a bookish man dedicated to academia with no desire to participate in wider society. Despite his intellect, Sir James believed that Daniel could try a little harder to fit in—even if he just endured it for the good of the family.

"So, Sir Rufus is just another aristocratic leech—his fading glory pushing him in my direction?" retaliated Daniel.

"He is a rather necessary leech I am afraid," Sir James Leicester retorted.

"Necessary to do what? Haven't you sufficient wealth already? You could start giving it away, and you could still afford to live like a king," he reprimanded his father. "And you want to sacrifice me to this 'has been'?" asked Daniel.

"Damn it!" his father yelled. "Why is it that you cannot show a shred of respect for the gentlemen who have made this country the great imperial power that it is today?" raged Sir James. "Sometimes, I wonder if you are my son!"

Daniel had heard that statement many times. As a child, it had hurt him, but as an adult, he accepted it as a compliment.

"An alliance with Sir Rufus will give us access to the House of Lords, Daniel. Have you any idea how that will empower us? With his background and connections, we will be able to establish an industrial footprint in the colonies," continued his father.

"Take a good look at Dianna. She is still a child," said Daniel fiercely. "I want a woman."

"She is of childbearing age, and I want an heir from you as soon as possible. You are thirty-five. If something should happen to you in one of those God-forsaken countries that you visit, you have no heir to claim your inheritance. I refuse to accept that my fortune will be lost because you won't marry and get on with it."

"My younger brothers have plenty of children. Leave it all to them," growled Daniel.

"Daniel, I was your age when I married your mother. You would not be on this earth if I had not fulfilled my duties, and I would have had no future if I had not married her."

"And how many months after your union was I born, father?"

His father looked at him with guilt. Daniel was touching a nerve. He was born two weeks prematurely, and in the early years of the Leicester marriage, it had concerned James that he was not the father of this wild child.

"I refuse to have a wife chosen on my behalf, father. Send the man and his daughter away," warned Daniel, his anger raising his voice.

The father was both taken aback and irritated by his son's petulant tone.

"It is admirable that you care for the girl's wellbeing. Most men of your age would be delighted by her pedigree, youth and beauty, even her innocence."

"And has she been given a choice in the matter, father? Or is she simply being prostituted out by Sir Rufus?"

The statement took his father off guard. *Will my eldest boy ever be capable of making a sensible decision?*

"Daniel, my son, think carefully. Now you are well into your thirties, think of the esteem that this union will bring you. You are no spring chicken. Choose a mistress and fall in love—if love is important to you. I am not expecting you to love your wife. You know as well as I do, marriage is a means to an end. It grants you status, and if you choose wisely—great wealth."

"Father, I am a man of independent means. I can support myself. I have already bought my own home in London without needing a penny from your estate. You will not dictate my life's path."

"If you humiliate this family with this headstrong attitude of yours, I will cut you out of my will, Daniel," roared Sir James Leicester, his fury now fully unleashed.

"So be it, father. Wealth and status are but a noose around my neck. We live in different times. What good is it to hold on to a fortune but not be able to live the life you wish or choose a woman you love. No, I will not do it. I would be signing up to a living death!"

Sir James Leicester became sullen. He wondered how he had succeeded in breeding this ingrate that had no respect for status and society. Sir James was disappointed in his eldest child. His son was a strong, educated and fearless man and often Sir James wished that Daniel was less self-sufficient, a little more dependent, so that he could wield a modicum of power over him.

2

THE LATE-NIGHT ENCOUNTER

The country house was teeming with young people. A thankful Daniel had so far succeeded in avoiding the frivolous weekend traditions that polite society designed to alleviate boredom. He kept himself to himself, dodged dinner on the first night and missed afternoon tea the following day.

Eventually, he received a note from his mother accusing him of being ill-mannered. To avoid her worsening wrath, he decided to try and please her.

Daniel Leicester was a dashing figure as he walked into the library. He was confident and distinguished and captured the attention of both men and women. Daniel was tall, healthy, athletic, rugged even, thanks to years of fresh air and outdoor activity.

Refusing to dress like a dandy, he wore an understated navy-blue jacket, free of frills and fancies, teamed with a pair of saggy, ill-fitting trousers. He timed his entrance to the minute, to avoid spending valuable time making boring conversation with Elizabeth's tiresome, giggly friends.

He towered above the pale and pasty men who were visiting for the weekend. They stood together in idle banter, their smooth, creamy faces and effeminate hands revealing their genteel upbringing.

Although the young women were eager to learn more about Elizabeth's eldest brother, they watched him from a distance. Secretly, however, they knew the attraction was one-sided—he was keen to make sure they knew he was out of their league.

Lady Leicester had gone to great lengths to ensure that the dining room was fit for royalty. The glass and silverware were polished until it sparkled as brightly as the crystal chandelier, the room's breathtaking centrepiece. It looked like a thousand twinkling stars cascading from the vaulted dining room ceiling.

The snow-white table cloths and napkins were crisp and starched, not a fold out of place. His mother looked regal in her formal gown and small tiara. She had seated him between Dianna Hamilton-Gordon and Erica McKenzie, a Scottish girl who had also attended boarding school with Elizabeth. Daniel sighed. Thinking it was demure, both young women tended to make minimal conversation. The place setting irritated Daniel.

He studied Dianna. Without a doubt, Sir Rufus was using her to bait his father's hook for some deal or other. Daniel wondered if the poor girl knew that he was targeted as the potential husband, the man with whom she would have to endure the rest of her life.

In terms of etiquette, the evening was successful. The conversation was light, the menu British and predictable. The meal was substantial and resulted in the ladies seeking repose in the large, echoing sitting room and the men moving on to the smoking room.

The smell of brandy and cigar smoke permeated the men's room. There was the low hum of deep voices, earnestly discussing the political situation of the day.

Daniel watched his father, now caught up in a debate with a young man called Churchill, the only person in the room who had anything interesting to say during the dinner. Desperate to withdraw, Daniel sat down beside the fireplace, poured a large brandy and reclined in a comfortable leather chair, staring at the dancing flames for solace. From the corner of his eye, he watched Rufus Hamilton-Gordon charm his way around the room. There was a lot of back-slapping, 'my dear fellows' and 'jolly good shows' until he reached Daniel.

"May I sit down?" enquired Sir Rufus.

It was seldom that the aristocracy appeared desperate and overly polite.

“Certainly,” said Daniel, pointing to the empty chair next to him, wondering when the odious chap would launch his play on him.

“The dinner was lovely,” began Sir Rufus.

“Yes, thank you. My mother is an excellent hostess.”

“I am glad that I have found you alone, Daniel. There is an important matter that I would like to discuss with you.” Sir Rufus paused and glanced around. “It is a sensitive subject.”

“Yes?”

“You are aware that your father and I have been discussing a joint venture, no doubt?” Sir Rufus stated.

“No, sir, I am not aware of it.”

“Well, then let me explain. It's rather simple old chap. The Suez Canal is under the jurisdiction of Great Britain. Our country is designing a defence strategy which will involve ships, cannon, transport and so on. I have access to this opportunity, and your father has access to cash to fund manufacturing capabilities. It will make us the wealthiest two men in Great Britain. Even the House of Saxe-Coburg may begin paying attention to us at last."

"Do you intend to create a new company for this—venture?" asked Daniel.

"No, we would like to form something stronger," Sir Rufus said with a subtle wink.

Daniel knew where the man was heading, but decided to enjoy watching Sir Rufus struggle to navigate the sensitive subject.

"You see, Sir James and I have agreed that you and Dianna would make a fine marriage alliance."

Sir Rufus stared into the fire, keen to avoid Daniel's steely glare.

"Oh, have you?"

"Yes, it will be all the security and collateral we need to build a fortune with no risk to either of us of ever losing it—or reneging on our commitment to each other."

Daniel did not respond, creating an uncomfortable silence between the two men.

"Daniel, my daughter is young enough to give you many children. She has many good years ahead of her."

Daniel nodded, absorbing the unwelcome information. He was unsurprised to learn the reason why his father and Sir Rufus had plotted their paths very carefully. Clearly, they had expected him to be seduced by the same lust for money and power that they were. Daniel Leicester was no prude, but he was sickened by the man's purely selfish ambitions, using his daughter as a honey trap.

"How does Dianna feel about this 'merger'?" asked Daniel.

"She is a compliant young woman, which should impress you. Dianna will do anything to improve our status, financial and otherwise. Since medieval times, it has been the purpose of marriage, has it not?"

"Mindless compliance is not a quality in a woman that appeals to me," Daniel scowled at the man.

"Your father has assured me of your participation."

"Has he?" said Daniel, his eyebrows racing up his forehead in surprise.

"Yes, he has committed to it, and I have committed my virtuous daughter to you," Sir Rufus smiled.

"Well, he has made a grave mistake. And so have you."

Daniel was furious that his father had the cheek to indulge Sir Rufus Hamilton-Gordon with promises on his behalf.

"Your father had guaranteed that no other woman will receive the Leicester name or fortune. I reciprocated by promising Sir James that no other man will win my daughter's title or virginity."

"Well, you seemed to have made a lot of plans on my—our— behalf," Daniel replied, his eyes looking vicious.

"Yes, of course, we have. Daniel, that is how dynasties are built in this country. We can announce the engagement immediately and then get on with planning the wedding," Sir Rufus said, confident that Daniel would agree with him.

"No, sir, you will not prepare for an engagement or a wedding ceremony. I do not wish to marry Dianna," Daniel complained. "I have no intention of procuring a wife in such a fashion."

"Now, now, you won't be procuring her, it will be a fair trade. I know you are an experienced man, and I will understand if you have reservations. However, you do not have to give up the free life that you are accustomed to. Dianna can stay in the countryside—and well, you can stay in London, if you prefer. I won't denounce a mistress if you need one later on, not that Dianna lacks skill in the bedroom," Sir Rufus suggested.

"No," said Daniel firmly, feeling rather awkward that the man was happy to eulogise so openly about his own daughter's carnal prowess.

"I assure you will not be disappointed by her. She is— mmm—charming."

Daniel stood up, and so did Sir Rufus. Daniel bent close to the little man. They stood almost nose to nose.

"You are a disgrace," Daniel said softly.

Sir Rufus did not know what to say. He was shocked by Daniel's candour.

Daniel could not tolerate the man near him any longer. He fought back a strong desire to punch him. Instead, he turned on his heels and left the room.

In the early hours of the morning, Daniel heard his bedroom door open softly. He could hardly hear the footsteps as the person crossed the room. She moved into the low firelight, and he saw that it was Dianna. She wore white nightclothes, and she moved to his bedside like a silent apparition.

"I have come to meet the man I am to marry," she whispered.

"I will not marry you, Dianna," he answered her harshly, hoping that she would go back to her own room.

"I don't care. I wanted you from the first moment that I saw you," she said, looking at him with large innocent eyes.

Daniel sighed.

"You are twenty-one. Dianna. There are other young men for you. What we do now will only break your heart," he said gently.

But his words did not hinder her. Instead of leaving, Dianna began to undress slowly. She climbed onto the bed next to Daniel, and she started to undress him as well. She demonstrated exceptional skill, and he lay back in shock as he began to experience remarkable pleasure. Despite her tender age, there was nothing more that he could teach her, and he soon learnt that she was most certainly not a virgin.

Dianna Hamilton-Gordon sat astride the body of Daniel Leicester. He lay beneath her like a god from the Greek myths. The sun had baked down upon his face and body, and his muscular arms glowed amber in the firelight. He had one huge bronzed hand on each of her hips and was carefully guiding her, she looked down at the dark hair on his chest that extended to his navel, and she became more aroused. Her gaze moved up to his dark eyes, and he smiled at her, his sensual mouth expressing his pleasure. His thick dark hair was closely clipped and framed his handsome, rugged face, each line and crease making him more masculine.

Dianna leaned forward and kissed him, her white skin touching his dark chest, and she was overwhelmed with a lustful desire. Alas, she felt no love for Daniel Leicester. Dianna was only fuelled by the longing for the wealth, power and status that his name could give her.

Daniel woke up with Dianna's head on his chest. Rather than the delight he felt after other romantic conquests, a despair settled over him, and he felt lonely and unfulfilled. Daniel peeled her from his body. She did not wake up, but burrowed deeper into the covers, her innocent face belying all of her experience.

Daniel put some logs onto the fire, then sat down and stared into the burning embers. He had just spent a night of passion with Dianna, whom he had been commanded to marry in the name of money, but the thought of spending a lifetime with a woman that he did not love terrified him.

Daniel watched the sleeping Dianna Hamilton-Gordon as she lay naked in his bed. He reflected on what had just happened. She had come to his bedroom and given him a night of passion. He remembered the way her luxurious hair fell around her face and rippled onto her snow-white skin. By his own admission, the girl was beautiful.

He sighed heavily. He had complicated his life by foolishly allowing her into his bed, and resentment engulfed him like a tidal wave. He knew that Dianna and her father were a conniving pair. He had compromised in the heat of passion and fallen for the oldest trap in the history of man. He had promised Dianna nothing, but guilt overwhelmed him; because while he was making love to Dianna Hamilton-Gordon, he was fantasizing that she was Catherine Frankland.

3

SURVIVING THE TENEMENT

Catherine 'Carter' as she now preferred to be known stood in the room she called home, surrounded by wet washing dripping water onto the cold floor. It could not have been any more removed from her Frankland family home. Her clothes hung from a makeshift washing line strung from corner to corner, and the coal stove was burning as hot as she could afford; but instead of drying the clothing, it just created steam, exacerbating the damp problem.

The flood of torrential rain had lasted for two weeks, making life even more difficult than it usually was in Whitechapel. Rainwater sloshed down the cobbles and formed a dam at the bottom of the street. It settled in big gloomy pools filled with the detritus it had collected on its journey down the slope. Rainwater also puthered in through the broken window pane in her room.

Catherine had worn the same clothing for three days and try as she may to keep it dry, it was beginning to stink in the humidity of the tiny room. The dampness risked the mildew worsening, and there was a risk of her getting sick again like she had been the year that she arrived in London. Her dire finances meant her hands were tied.

Not long after she had arrived in Whitechapel, the doctor had diagnosed her with pneumonia. He kept her in hospital for four weeks. Catherine had been desperately ill, and although the hospital was hardly paradise, the bed was dry and warm, and she managed to recover.

She was depressed when the doctor discharged her. All she had to look forward to was the day to day struggle to survive. Catherine had no choice. The option of going back to her home in sleepy Lymington nestled on the Hampshire coastline was gone forever after she fled her husband.

On the positive side, her illness was how she first met her neighbour, Janey. Catherine remembered the day clearly. It was a dismal winter's morning, and the cold neutralised the little bit of warmth radiated by her coal stove. She had coughed all night, and her lungs burnt like fire. A fever had started to take hold, and she had struggled through the night, hoping to feel better by morning. However, it got worse. Catherine was struggling to breathe.

Janey had lain listening to the neighbour's laboured breathing all night. She had heard the rasping sound before when her mother had died of pneumonia. It gave her a tremendous empathy for the girl next door. They had only greeted each other in passing. Catherine was a private person, and Janey could see that she was not from those parts. She couldn't help but keep an eye on the newcomer.

By lunchtime, her inquisitive neighbour grew concerned and knocked loudly on Catherine's door.

Catherine could not decide whether she should open the door or not but eventually willed herself out of bed. Her sleep-deprived body was stiff. Each step was painful.

In her drowsy state, she unlocked the door without looking to see who it was. Exhausted and delirious, Catherine turned around and trundled back to her bed.

Once in repose, she opened her eyes slightly to see who was there— the woman looked familiar.

> "Sorry to bother you lass, I am Janey, yer
> neighbour like, but I haven't seen ye all day,
> and usually yer up on yer toes before sunrise.
> I heard yer coughing all night, love. How are
> ye feeling?"

Catherine didn't have the strength or desire to answer. At a glance, Janey knew that Catherine was deathly sick and that she would be beyond help if she could not get her to the hospital quickly.

"What is yer name then, Missy?" asked Janey.

"Catherine," she wheezed, unable to move without coughing uncontrollably.

"Come on, then, Catherine. I have a bit of money. We will get to the market square and take a cart to the hospital."

"I can't take your money, Janey," rasped Catherine, barely able to speak.

"Oh, stop with that talk, my girl. Don't yer worry about that now. I did good business last night. I can afford it."

"Thank you," Catherine mouthed.

"Now, let's be gone, lass," said Janey encouragingly. "No use yer getting that consumption and all. Let's get yer over to that hospital and be done with it. Come on now, Catherine, yer will be dead by nightfall if ye don't hurry. Time to choose between the hearse and the hospital, lass! Come on."

Janey patiently helped Catherine out of bed and dressed her as warmly as she could, then guided her down the dirty staircase and onto the street. Walking toward the market, Catherine's knees were prone to buckling, and she collapsed twice as they struggled on. Each time, Janey had a hard battle to get the invalid back to her feet.

Rather than assist, strangers walked past the two women as though they did not exist.

Janey was still there for her friend when Catherine returned from the hospital, and she took it upon herself to nurse her back to full health.

> "I always wanted to be a nurse," Janey confessed as she propped Catherine up with one hand giving her pillow a thump with the other. "But that bloody Nightingale woman didn't want to accept me cos she got wind that I flashed me thruppennies occasionally."

Despite Janey's cheery banter, Catherine's mind was elsewhere. She noticed how tired and depressed she felt. So deep was the melancholy, it was the only time that she had felt tempted to return to her horrid husband's house in Hampshire.

During the long cold nights on the road to recovery, Catherine and Janey shared many a secret. These moments of closeness were the catalyst for what was to become a life-long friendship.

> "Yer a bloody fool now if yer even considers going back to that devil," swore Janey.

> "I was stupid to leave him. Why did I think I could survive here, Janey? I've gone out of the frying pan into the fire," snivelled Catherine.

"You were brave to leave. I reckon if you go back, you will never have peace, lass. Things will get better, you'll see. I can feel it in my bones. You'll find a better-paid job, and soon you will be able to afford something a lot nicer than this hovel. Why don't yer write to your parents? They love yer, don't they?"

"I can't. My husband will ruin them. They should know nothing. I might send a letter one day, so they know that I am safe. The thought of that will have to do for now."

Catherine was full of self-pity. It was Janey who gave her hope to carry on. One day there would be a brighter future for her. *One day.*

Janey looked after her day and night, except when she had the occasional gentleman visitor. She had created a little goldmine servicing a few good men in the area. There were only five chaps on her books, and they were from the better side of Whitechapel.

Janey explained that she had handpicked her clientele. Her regulars were clean and decent fellows. She stated to Catherine that two of the men were widowers. Two others were young red-blooded chaps eager for a 'regular roll in the hay and a good laugh'. The final one was a surprising choice—a Catholic priest.

"A priest!" Catherine exclaimed.

> "Now, Missy, don't yer be judging," Janey said sternly. "Would you prefer him to take his natural instincts out on young girls—or boys?"

Catherine looked at her with an equally puzzled and disappointed frown.

> "See lass, when these lads are sixteen and decide to become priests, it is a safe haven for them. But, when they don't have that lifelong calling to be a pious clergyman, they grow to have physical desires like all of us. It is a decent red-blooded bloke who finds a woman like me instead of abusing little choir boys," she chuckled darkly.

Catherine would smile fondly as she remembered her friend. *Praise the dear Lord for Janey, because as wild as she is, she has been a pillar of strength and a source of humour on the best and worst of days.* She knew without a doubt that it was Janey's unwavering support that had kept her alive.

With the damp clothes now folded in a pile on the bed, Catherine stood in front of a basin of steaming water. She washed her hands and face, as her persistent cough returned. The hot water warmed her skin briefly, but the soap suds stung her chilblains. She hoped that it would stop raining. Not that it would change the dour atmosphere in Whitechapel that much. It seemed to be in a constant twilight of suffocating misery.

Hearing the coughing, Janey knocked on Catherine's door and let herself in without waiting for the invite.

"Ye Gods, Catherine!" Janey exclaimed. "Just look at this place, me darlin'," she said, looking at the broken window and the worsening mould. "Come with me. My bed is dry. We can share for the night."

Catherine accepted graciously. Three years ago, she wouldn't even have considered the invitation, but this was Whitechapel, and she had developed an acute gratitude for places that were warm and dry.

They climbed onto Janey's bed, each clutching a hot cup of tea. Despite it being adulterated with floor sweepings by the unscrupulous owner at the char factory, it tasted reasonable.

"Now tell me, lass. What's it like to be rich?"

"It's the same as being poor, Janey. It's difficult to get away from, and it doesn't make you happy."

"But surely it's better than being a poor wretch like you are now? Those big houses are all warm, clean and dry. Plus, there's plenty of food and drink, isn't there?"

"Yes, that's true. But there is very little freedom," replied Catherine. "Especially for women."

"But surely with all that money, yer can do what yer want?"

"No," laughed Catherine. "When you get married—to a man chosen by your family—your husband gets your money, and you no longer have any financial independence."

"So yer're tellin' me, that all 'em high fallutin' ladies are poor?"

"Well," giggled Catherine, "yes, I suppose that they are, in a sense. They're looked after by their husbands, of course, but they don't have access to their own money to make their own choices. They have no free will."

"And you, lass? Can you look after yerself, like? It seems to me you're struggling more and more, despite being able to find work?"

"I am looking after myself to the best of my ability, Janey, just like you. But, it seems you are far more successful than me."

Both women burst into giggles.

"I can give yer an apprenticeship with these fellas if yer want, lass?"

"I think I'll pass on that kind offer." Catherine laughed out loud.

"So, what happened to all yer money, then?"

"It belongs to my husband now."

"Just like that, lass? So, all these toffs steal the money from their wives?"

"Not according to the law, they don't," laughed Catherine, "but yes, some of them only get rich when they marry and receive their wife's money."

"And here I was finking them sirs are better than us."

"No, Janey. At the end of it all, we are all the same. The rich just wear prettier clothes and live in nicer homes."

Catherine had endured several menial jobs during her Whitechapel years. At first, she got fired for insubordination. By now, she had learnt a lot—primarily to shut her mouth and mind her own business. Speaking out of turn achieved nothing.

Desperately hungry and one week away from finally becoming destitute, recently, she found a job with Mrs Watson, a local seamstress. Watson had six women working for her, who became a small sisterhood in times of trouble. As an employer, Mrs Watson was patient and relished in teaching Catherine because she was quick and thorough. Never in her wildest dreams did she think that those boring embroidery lessons at her old family home would ever come in handy to keep a roof over her head.

Catherine had worked there for almost two years. Her overheads were such that her wages hardly lasted the week, but at least it was regular work. Her clothes were mended and re-mended. However, the work environment was warm and dry, and Mrs Watson gave them one meal of hot broth a day which was of great benefit when she was flat broke. Sadly, the ageing Mrs Watson had recently perished from a heart attack, and unfortunately for Catherine, her seamstress job died with her.

Catherine had put in a bid for the small company with the other girls, but Mrs Watson was in debt, and the bank recovered it from her estate. The business lost all her sewing machines. After that, the landlord unlocked the premises and greedily rifled through the desk and took the poor old woman's order book and customers with him.

Newly jobless and without a penny of savings to her name, Catherine was in dire financial straits. If Janey had not offered to help her, she would have been off to the workhouse.

It was a miracle that Catherine found a job as a housekeeper within days. Help was needed five days a week. She had read the advertisement in the newspaper and walked to the employment office for an interview. She had no qualifications or references for the role, but the woman who interviewed her was impressed that Catherine could read, write and do arithmetic. She felt those qualities could be beneficial to the client, a professor, who needed help in his household. The woman quickly realised that Catherine was bright and well-spoken. She did not ask the applicant too many questions about her past, afraid that it may seem that she was prying, but she was confident that Catherine was from an affluent family, and had fallen on hard times. She made an offer on the spot, which was gleefully accepted.

Catherine rushed home to tell Janey the news of her success after buying two gloriously gooey iced cinnamon buns to celebrate. She invited Janey into her room and ushered her confidante onto her rickety fireside chair.

> "Can you imagine me as a professor's housekeeper, Janey? I don't know where to start," laughed Catherine as she handed the sticky sweet treat to her friend.

> "I can imagine him, a bespectacled little man with an odd bow tie, smoking a pipe at the desk in his study, floor-to-ceiling bookcases, and being ever-so-slightly pompous."

Janey mimed the scene playing out in her head.

> "Ah, Miss Carter, bring me my afternoon tea, and don't spill it all in the saucer this time."

Janey roared with laughter, almost dropping the remains of the bun.

"But hats off te yer me sweetheart, not many refined women like you would lower themselves to be a maid. Let me give yer some tips, petal. If yer famished and need to sneak some food, only take small amounts at a time—or they'll notice."

Catherine shook her head and smiled.

"I am not going to steal from him, Janey."

"Don't use the word steal, Catherine, 'a permanent loan' is a better way of putting it."

"You are shocking, Janey," chuckled Catherine, thoroughly entertained by her madcap friend.

"If you are going to use his bath and wash, make sure that everything is dry when he gets back."

"Oh, Janey, that is outrageous."

"Tis not! In the dead of winter, a hot bath is a luxury!" she protested in jest.

"Oh, and money—nick notes rather than the silver. They never believe that you're brazen enough to pocket a note, but they always check the coins," advised Janey in a hushed tone, leading Catherine to believe her friend must have been a professional pilferer at some point.

"One last thing, lass. Don't skulk about quietly when you are pinching stuff. Be as bold as brass. Make a lot of noise in the vicinity of the loot. It will confuse them."

"Janey, you are incorrigible," sighed a bemused and somewhat concerned Catherine. "—So, have you pulled a stunt like this yourself?"

"Nah, lass. But me aunty did. Regular like. She worked as a chambermaid in a big posh house. She taught me everything. Very clever, she was. Besides, who's to know. One day you might need to use this little tip," said Janey with a face grinning broader than a Cheshire cat.

Janey shut the door behind her, still chuckling. Catherine shook her head and smiled.

Moments later, there was another knock at the door. Janey had returned.

"Close your eyes. Put your hands out. Now, cup them."

A confused Catherine did as she was told. Janey tumbled a few coins into her outstretched hands.

"You nip out to the market and see if you can get some clothes that aren't more repair patch than fabric. It'll tide you over until you get your uniform."

A thankful Catherine grasped the coins as a lump formed in her throat. *I am lucky to have such a friend.*

Catherine left for Mayfair daunted by the impressive address. She was surprised to find that the entrance to the apartment was at the back of an imposing old mansion. She collected the key from another employee, Mr Farley. The kindly old man would have kept her talking all day if she had allowed it. He was a cheerful chap with sparkling bright blue eyes. The roguish twinkle told Catherine he must have been a delightfully mischievous little boy.

"Aha, so you must be the professor's new maid," welcomed Mr Farley cheerfully.

"Yes. Miss Catherine Carter," she said nervously.

"Do you know how many days will you be coming in?" asked Mr Farley.

"Five days a week, Sir."

"Good," said Mr Farley with a smile. "You are going to have some unusual responsibilities, Miss Carter."

"How so?" asked a frowning Catherine.

"Nothing too unusual," replied the man noting her concern.

"As you probably know from your interview, since the professor lectures at the University of London, he travels the world to stay at the top of his field. You must be highly educated to work here and look after the place in his absence."

"I may be poor, Mr Farley," she answered, "but, I assure you I am not stupid. I am aware of the basic principles of the academic world."

Mr Farley laughed, which seemed to irritate Catherine, rather than lighten the mood as he had hoped.

"That apartment of his is littered with remnants and relics from his travels. He has books piled to the ceiling. His only demand is that when caring for these items, nothing is damaged."

The description sounded like her father's home. Catherine nodded, convinced that Farley was exaggerating the chaos that lay within.

"It is your job to keep everything neat and clean, of course, but also to report any signs of deterioration. All those old bits and pieces he keeps may begin to decay when they are not stored properly in their protective glass cases, or so the professor told me. He has left detailed instructions on his desk."

Catherine nodded. *The agency mentioned nothing of this. I thought my typical duties would be day to day cleaning of the house, not be an underpaid museum curator!* Despite the revelation, she smiled to herself. She was in familiar territory—her father was also an archaeologist. She knew better than to disclose her identity to anybody and made a mental note never to mention the name Frankland in front of the professor.

"Will you need help with the letter?" asked Mr Farley delicately.

"Thank you, Mr Farley. I will be fine. Rest assured, I will pipe up if I need you."

"Right then, Miss Carter. I'll let you make a start. There is a lot that needs attention, as you can probably imagine. My wife and I live in the attic. Call me if you need help. See you later, perhaps?"

He smiled as he watched her tentatively climb the steps to the apartment door. From her gait and accent, Mr Farley recognised that she was not originally from the impoverished part of London that she now seemed to reside in. There was more to her backstory than she was letting on. Nevertheless, he was sure that the professor would like her. She was clearly bright and spirited.

Catherine unlocked the heavy door and stepped into a cluttered hallway. The black and white marble floor was strewn with books piled high on the furniture. It was evident that nobody had cleaned for weeks. A thick layer of dust covered everything. The apartment smelled of old books and leather, but not in a pleasant way. There was an unpleasant mustiness about the place because the windows had clearly not been opened for some time.

After watching her step as she crossed the teetering piles of obstacles, Catherine opened the door to what appeared to be a sitting room and dining room in one. The room had a masculine atmosphere. A well-used leather couch was positioned in front of a large fireplace. The rest of the furniture was pushed tightly against the wall to make space for the many strange artefacts from distant lands. Catherine wished that her father was with her. He would have delighted in delving through the bits and pieces lying around the room.

She moved forward to take a closer look at some labels tied onto the objects with twine. Ethiopia, Palestine, Egypt. She recognised the names of many exotic places, but there were also some that she had never heard of before.

Catherine opened a door that led to a bedroom dominated by a colossal four-poster bed, made of carved ebony columns. The wood was pitch black underneath a thick coating of dust. It promised to be beautiful when it was clean. The appearance suggested was definitely a man's bedroom, not a couple's. It was also the only orderly space she had seen so far. All the other pieces of bedroom furniture were as exotic as the bed. The soft furnishings were made of ethnic fabrics, displaying colours and patterns so vibrant that they would have been considered vulgar by some of her peers.

She tiptoed into the study, which was the largest room in the apartment. In the centre was a round table with six chairs arranged haphazardly around it. At the far end was an imposing mahogany desk the size of a small courtyard in Whitechapel. An oak swivel chair stood behind that desk, this time pushed neatly underneath. Two large armchairs, with plush crimson velvet upholstery, were placed in front of the fireplace. *If I'm not mistaken, they are resting on top of a Middle Eastern dhurrie rug.* She touched it inquisitively—*yes, unmistakably camel hair.*

Catherine braced herself before entering the kitchen, expecting it to be the worst room. To delay the inevitable, she sat down behind the mahogany desk and found the note Farley had mentioned. On the crisp envelope, some words had been handwritten with a flourish: *'To the Housekeeper.'*

She opened the letter and found a quickly scrawled, barely legible note inside.

> *Dear Miss Carter,*
>
> *I trust that you know how to clean a house.*

Please dust throughout, but do not move anything.

I will meet you here in person on Monday week at eight AM sharp to discuss your role and responsibilities.

A flamboyantly signed name marked the end of the note, but it was unreadable. Looking at the thick coating of dust around her, Catherine set to work.

Catherine was taken aback when Monday week arrived. Although the amount of careful cleaning work required to get the apartment shipshape had been painstakingly slow, the week itself had still flown by surprisingly quickly.

An anxious Catherine Carter arrived at the Mayfair apartment just before eight o'clock. It had been enjoyable working alone for a week, but now it was bound to be different. The professor would be at home, no doubt scrutinising everything that she did. *What will he be like? I do hope he is agreeable.* Catherine prayed that she had not misplaced anything while she was cleaning. *That would be a ghastly way to start the relationship.*

As she walked up the path to the servant's entrance Mr Farley, on the lookout for her arrival from his attic window, leapt into action and rushed downstairs to greet her.

"Good morning, Miss Carter."

"Morning," she replied courteously.

"He is home," Farley whispered as he escorted her up the stairs to the door. "Good luck, Miss."

Catherine took a deep breath as she put the key into the lock and let herself in. She noted that all the doors and windows were wide open and that the morning sunlight and fresh air was streaming into the formerly stuffy rooms. The professor had taken no care when he opened the floor-length drapes and had simply pushed everything to one side, rather than leaving the fabric neatly arranged in tidy folds as she had done.

Some sturdy brown work boots lay in front of the sitting room fireplace, and there was an empty whisky glass on the table.

She made her way through to the kitchen and saw a small copper pot with a long handle bubbling away on the stove. It permeated the air with the most delightful smell of coffee.

Catherine stepped into the study. A man sat behind the large desk, his dark head bent over. He was lost in his own world, examining a curious stone object in his hand. She gave a light knock on the door to signal her arrival, but there was still no response.

"Ahem. Good morning, Professor," said Catherine politely.

Again, he didn't answer her. Instead, he lifted a magnifying glass continuing to scrutinise whatever it was that he was holding. Catherine stood in silence for quite some time and then accepted that he was distracted and did not want to talk to her. She turned around to leave when a deep voice boomed at her.

"Good morning, Miss Carter. Off so soon?"

The professor still did not look up from what he was doing.

"No, Sir. Good morning, Sir."

There was no reply.

"Can I make you tea, Sir?" asked Catherine out of habit. Feeling flustered, it was the only polite thing she could think of to break the frosty atmosphere. Alas, she instantly felt foolish and inattentive because she had just seen the coffee on the stove.

"Coffee would be nice," he answered as he turned the object over in his hand.

"Yes, Sir."

"Oh, and for heaven's sake, Miss Carter," he said, "let's lose all this stuffy formality from the outset. May I call you Catherine, it is your name after all?"

"Of course, Sir," she stammered.

He looked up for the first time since she had come into the room.

"I am—"

He began, but could not finish the sentence, because in front of him stood a woman he had not seen for years. She had made quite an impression on him, yet he had given up on ever seeing her again. She took two steps forward to see him clearly and found herself staring at the face of a ruggedly handsome familiar face. She knew him immediately. *Daniel Leicester—the man who breezed into my life and changed it forever.*

"Catherine," he nodded. It was a statement, not a question.

"Yes."

"When did you become 'Catherine Carter?'"

"Three years ago," she answered.

"Did you remarry?" he asked in a deep unemotional voice.

"No. I changed my name."

"And now a rich girl like you is a housemaid?" he snarled.

"Yes."

"Where are you living?"

"Whitechapel."

"Humph. I see. So, you are 'slumming it'?" he chuckled cruelly at his crude play on words.

"Are you always this rude?" said Catherine, unable to stifle the defensive reply.

"Yes, I probably am."

"It's a place where my husband can't find me."

"Ah, so you are still married then. Let me guess—it didn't work out?"

"No."

"Any plans to divorce him?"

"No. He doesn't know where I am. That will have to do for now."

He looked up at her.

"I can understand that it would upset a man if his wife ran away, making him think she were dead."

"I don't need to explain anything to you, Daniel."

"I see you despite the new name, you are still the same feisty old Catherine, never needing to explain anything to anyone."

She did not grace him with a response.

"Come," he said, suddenly changing his tone. "I am brewing a pot of Turkish coffee on the stove. I will show you how to make it. Tea is frightfully overrated. Oh, and don't worry about breakfast. I will tell you if I'm hungry—"

He paused for a second.

"Mrs Conacher, my previous housekeeper worked here for six years. Eventually, I had to retire her. She was too elderly to continue. It was time for her to rest. She had worked her whole life," said Daniel, with no reference to what happened to the poor old woman.

He showed Catherine the small copper pot on the stove. She was inches from him. Nothing had changed—he was still the most attractive man she had ever met.

"You just put everything in the pot. Add three heaped spoons of this coffee, then three of sugar. Once it comes to the boil, pour it into these little cups. It's the best coffee you will ever drink," he explained.

He showed no signs of emotion or affection. He was simply giving her instructions. After rolling his sleeves up, he prepared the drink he had started earlier. She watched his manly hands as he worked.

When he finished pouring, he handed Catherine her drink, then made his way towards the kitchen door with his. He took a mouthful of coffee, as he stopped to turn round to look at her. Catherine held her breath. Was this the moment she was waiting for—a longing that he would acknowledge their shared past?

> "Oh, and, for God's sake Catherine, don't move anything or I will never find it again. Just dusting and continue doing what housekeepers do."

Everything felt painfully awkward for both of them.

She felt relief a short while later when he announced that he was going to the university. She noted that he dressed like somebody from Whitechapel. His grey baggy trousers were as simple as the ones that she saw on the workers, and his well-worn tweed jacket had patches at the elbows. On top of his handsome head was a battered brown fedora hat.

Although the quality of his clothing was appalling for a gentleman of his calibre, he still managed to look sophisticated to her—as if a tailor had made the outfit on Savile Row. It was not the clothes that made him the man he was, but his quiet confidence and the as yet untamed sense of freedom.

Daniel Leicester walked to the University of London in a daze. He could not focus on anything. His mind became a sieve. The name of the person he was supposed to meet eluded him, and he had to look it up in his diary.

The last person he had expected to return to his life that morning was Catherine Frankland. It was several years since he last saw her, but there wasn't one day that she escaped his dreams or his memory. Before he met her, Daniel believed that love was a myth. He had no desire to get married since she vanished, but he and Catherine Frankland had connected on a level he never imagined possible. He was convinced, that despite their rocky relationship, she was the only woman he wanted to spend the rest of his life with.

4

THE CONFESSION

As Daniel walked to the Faculty of Archaeology, he shook his head and smiled faintly, remembering the first time that he met Catherine. It had all started with a weekend invitation to the Frankland Estate in Lymington. Little did he know that encounter would forever change his life.

He thought back to sitting in his faculty office, cold, miserable and bored. Whilst he loved academic pursuits, he detested the politics that accompanied it. He found it frustrating that he must spend a term lecturing bone-idle students if he wanted the university to finance his next research project.

He managed his boredom best by planning his next expedition. It was tiresome lecturing privileged youths who saw archaeology merely as a gateway to adventure, rather than respecting the history and science that was the foundation of the subject. For Daniel, archaeology was most certainly not the modern equivalent of an excuse for a spoilt young man to embark on a hedonistic seventeenth-century 'grand tour'.

He had one hundred and twenty-three papers to mark. Except for two promising students whose work he liked to leave til last, the remainder showed no signs of talent whatsoever. With a heavy heart, he took another lacklustre submission from the pile.

By lunchtime, Daniel was starving for intellectual stimulation just as much as food. He took himself off to the dining hall to find his friend, Javier Fernando, a Spanish archaeologist who specialised in South American regions.

"I have to get out of this place, Javier. Compared with a dig, it is miserable cooped in these dark and dismal rooms. My tutees are nothing more than a bunch of ingrates. At times it has me wishing I had become a carpenter or a fisherman or maybe even a farmer. Anything but a blasted archaeologist," Daniel growled.

"Oh, my friend, Daniel. Si, si, señor. England may have a proud academic history, but it has no soul. Now, my country, it has soul. We live in the sunshine, as happy, vibrant and passionate people, exploring the finer things in life."

"I hate to agree with you," sighed Daniel.

"Where are you going for the weekend, Señor Daniel?" asked Javier, hoping to change the subject.

"I have an invitation to the Frankland estate for his annual lecture, but the dean has threatened me with my job if I do not tutor the young and hapless Duxbury in deciphering Greek. The chap is as thick as a brick. What he is doing at university is a mystery."

"No, no, my friend. I am sure we can assign another poor fellow to tutor Duxberry. It will be easy to find a replacement, for I don't think there is a man on earth that knows less about Greek than Duxberry!"

Daniel's face brightened up at the suggestion of a substitute.

"I too have an invitation. I believe the keynote speaker is giving a lecture on Mary Anning and her palaeontological work on the Jurassic coast."

Daniel rested his head in his hands and groaned.

"I am not a fossil collector, Javier, I am an archaeologist. Looking at those confounded stones with their dreary shells embedded within is more boring than marking endless essays," he sighed. "Nevertheless, the Franklands have helped me a lot in the past, so I must show my gratitude."

"Si, I feel the same way about palaeontology. Still, it will get us out of here for a few days. Some sea air will do us both good," Javier cajoled as he lightly punched Daniel's arm.

When the weekend finally arrived, the two academics hurriedly packed their suitcases and bought their tickets to Lymington. It was a cold, dark and wintery afternoon, and the storm clouds gathered as they travelled south. Both men were eager to reach their destination. The train thundered past miles of inky black landscape, only stopping for passengers to alight at pretty little stations, each butter-coloured building richly bathed in a warm yellowy gaslit glow.

Gazing absentmindedly out of the window, Daniel experienced a sense of nostalgia. He recalled the long overseas journeys he had made to far-flung dig sites. *The pinnacle of adventure is being unaware of what lies ahead.* This unpredictable lifestyle satisfied the personal freedom he craved and fuelled the professional passion for his chosen academic career—at least when he was not spoon-feeding indolent students.

The Frankland house, built with local limestone, stood above the rocky, rugged coastline, proudly overlooking the sea. In the light of the full moon, the building shone like a phantom in the pitch dark of night. He could see the steel grey Solent from the road, and he relished the smell of the sea.

The vast estate was unlike other gloomy manor houses that he had visited. The gardens were immaculate and colourful. Inside it was an eclectic mixture oriental furniture and traditional English oak panelling. It was a delightful place, and it had a warm and welcoming atmosphere that Daniel enjoyed.

The two weary travellers were welcomed like royalty. Their suitcases and coats were politely taken from them. A welcome drink was thrust into their hand, and they were ushered towards some winged Chesterfields in the parlour. Tired from their journey, they collapsed in silence preferring to savour the sips of spirit, feeling the burning liquid tingle down their throats.

Feeling a little more refreshed after their drinks, the men were shown to their rooms. Each one found a note on their pillows informing them there would be a reception in the library at eight o'clock, the dress code formal. For once, Daniel panicked about his appearance, wondering what state his formalwear would be in after being squashed in his suitcase for several hours.

He needn't have been concerned. As he looked around his room, he spotted his black dinner suit and white wing-collared shirt hanging on a clothes rack next to his suitcase. His clothing had been neatly pressed, and his patent-leather shoes were polished to shine like mirrors. He smiled to himself. *The Frankland household is clearly a tight run ship!*

After he had washed, shaved and dressed, he looked at his elegant reflection in the mirror. *It seems I can scrub up well.* Leaving his bedroom with a chuckle, he made his way downstairs, occasionally stopping to examine the swathes of interesting artefacts and paintings that adorned the walls and alcoves.

The library resembled Daniel's later Mayfair apartment. The shelves were packed solid. Elsewhere in the room, most of the flat surfaces had a tall and wobbly pile of books teetering above them. Collections of artefacts were peppered throughout the room. There was no particular order to the arrangement that anyone else would understand except a fellow archaeologist. The room was crowded with men and their wives, chatting politely. Some he recognised as well-respected academics; others were strangers to him.

Sir Herbert Frankland stood speaking to a small group of men who appeared to concentrate on his every word, nodding their heads in agreement at whatever he was telling them.

Frankland was a world-renowned archaeologist, highly respected in his field. For years, he had promoted the fossil-rich south coast as a place worthy of detailed study and written many books on the subject. His expertise was sought all over the world. Daniel Leicester was in awe of him.

Academics in England were going through a time of considerable uncertainty. The Labour Party resented financing archaeologists to dig up other people's countries, and the Conservatives resented that more women were taking up the subject. Daniel had returned from many meetings in Westminster, battle-weary and discouraged, longing for a rewarding career, 'untainted by blessed politics'. Sir Herbert used his wealth and status to become a great advocate for the sciences. Further, he had spent a significant amount of time and effort endorsing Daniel's next survey.

Although Frankland was supportive in the political world, Daniel enjoyed him more out in the field. They had spent months together in the hot sun, sleeping under starlit skies. Over many glasses of gin and tonic, they researched and documented their findings, indulging their mutual passion for archaeology. Daniel knew Frankland had a family because the man often spoke about his sons. It seemed he also had a rarely mentioned daughter.

The vast library was well lit. Shards of light also reflected off the silverware, creating ethereal patterns on the bookshelves. The two hearths that graced each end of the room held roaring fires that warmed everyone. The comfort of the library was a core element of the welcoming atmosphere for their guests. Large crystal chandeliers hung from the high ceilings, illuminated by electricity rather than gas. In the few rooms that were no full to bursting with books and artefacts, the walls were covered with ancient tapestries depicting images of love and war from bygone eras.

A tall well-groomed and immaculately dressed man, Daniel Leicester stood head and shoulders above the others in the room. Gazing around the assembled throng, he identified some of his fellow academics and made a mental note to avoid them. *I am in no mood to discuss politics or work.* If he got tangled up in a conversation with them, he knew they would speak about nothing else. Some men took pleasure in relaying the same experiences again and again. Daniel refused to indulge them. Instead, he made for the shadows in an attempt to go unnoticed.

Settled into a dark corner, that was when he first saw her.

The beautiful Catherine Frankland stood at the centre of the room, looking imperious. She wore a simple sleeveless pink evening gown, embroidered with grey thread and small grey pearls. Instead of her flowing hair being pinned and plaited, her hair hung down her back and shined in the light. Her grey eyes sparkled as she laughed. A group of young fops gathered around her delightedly. Smooth-skinned and well-educated, they were the type who spent the better part of their days reading poetry and lounging about the homes of their wealthy parents. Although the young men were captivated by Catherine's beauty and eloquence, she was bored and wished that somebody would rescue her.

Sir Herbert always kept a keen eye on his daughter, and at a glance, he sensed her discomfort. He excused himself from a conversation with a grey-haired matronly-looking woman, walked over to Catherine and took her arm.

"Thank you, Father," she whispered, in his ear.

"Where is your fiancé this time?" he asked with irritation.

"I don't know, Father. I expect he is in conversation with somebody else."

"It is time Sebastian Pimbleby took care of you at these social events. I can't look after you forever. I wish you were married already, Catherine."

Catherine frowned but did not comment.

"I always have to save you from those unsavoury characters who flock around you like vultures," he grumbled. "It leaves me no time to have fun. Where are your brothers when I need them?"

Sir Herbert escorted Catherine across the room, and every eye was upon her. It made him feel like a king. His spirited daughter was the apple of his eye, but he worried about her. Of the eligible suitors her father had suggested, he felt she had made a poor choice in a husband. No matter how hard Herbert tried to dissuade her from marrying the abhorrent Pimbleby, she refused to change her mind. Even as a child, Catherine had been obstinate, but this was ridiculous. *What she sees in Sebastian is a mystery.*

Daniel, now leaning against a pillar, was almost invisible. Quaffing his host's finest scotch, he had started to relax. However, even with his considerable effort to go unseen, Sir Herbert spotted him and steered Catherine in his direction. Daniel straightened up from his relaxed pose.

"Good evening, old friend," said Sir Herbert Frankland as he put out his hand.

Catherine watched the two men greet each other, trying to recall who the handsome man was, although she was reasonably sure she'd never encountered him before.

"Good evening, Herbert," replied Daniel. To Catherine, his voice sounded like a rich deep purr.

"You must be relieved to be home," joked Frankland.

"Hardly!" laughed Daniel. "England is far too cold."

Herbert gave a wry smile.

"I don't think you've met my daughter, Catherine?"

Daniel nodded a greeting and returned to his conversation with her father. Catherine studied him carefully. *He is tall, dignified and carries himself well.*

"Thank you for your support this year," said Daniel with a smile. "Thanks to your influence in parliament, our next expedition is approved."

His conversation had none of the trivialities she normally heard young men of her age witter on about. She could see her father's deep respect for him as their conversation moved from academia to farming. Catherine was so used to men fawning over her, yet Daniel made no attempt to include her in the conversation. She found it curious he had not acknowledged her presence at all apart from that first nod of greeting.

The conversation continued about cattle and sheep sales, and it was annoying Catherine immensely. She was close to excusing herself when her father saw an entourage of Arab sheiks enter the library.

"Please excuse me, Daniel, that is Sheikh Fahad from Abu Dhabi, I have to greet him and take him into a more private setting—the Arabs are very sensitive."

"Please do."

"Daniel, would you mind keeping my daughter company until her fiancé finds her? He seems to have disappeared—again."

Catherine was left standing next to Professor Daniel Leicester. Alone, with a more mature man, she lost all her bravado and could find nothing intelligent to discuss. For Daniel, the idea of being a chaperone was torture, but he stood stoically at his post, wondering when her fiancé would notice that she was missing.

"So your name is Catherine?"

"Yes," she answered. "Lady Catherine Rebecca Frankland. It's a bit of a mouthful."

Her attempt to forge a conversation failed. Daniel said nothing in reply, preferring to nod as he took a slow sip of his liquor. The silence was excruciating for Catherine, but Daniel was comfortable with the icy atmosphere. After some time, he asked her how old she was.

"Twenty-two," she replied.

"Are you planning to get married soon?"

"Soon. It has been a long engagement."

"Why are you marrying? Aren't there better things to do at your age—as a woman of means? You are still quite young."

Her eyes widened in anger, and she looked the other way.

"May I ask what his name is?"

"Sebastian Pimbleby."

"Oh, that little upstart! Your father knows a lot of men with sons. I am sure that he could arrange someone better."

"I'll have you know Sebastian comes from a well-respected family. That is why I agreed to our engagement."

"Aah, so you chose him?"

"Yes, I did, and I do not have to explain myself to you."

Daniel stifled a belly laugh.

"My father did not choose my fiancé. It was my own decision, Professor Leicester."

"You should have left it to your father, you might have fared better."

Her long eyelashes fluttered, and her large grey eyes twinkled up at him. He could see the fire and the passion in those eyes. Catherine's full lips pouted in irritation. He ignored it, and he went on to take note of the curves of her figure under her dress. Her skin looked smooth and soft, and he wanted to touch it.

"Do you think my father would have chosen you?" she asked coolly.

Lacking some refinement, he blundered:

"Oh, God, I hope not."

He laughed, taking a mouthful of whisky to avoid having to speak again. Catherine blushed scarlet.

"Would you want somebody to choose your partner, Daniel?"

"I suppose not."

At last, the uncomfortable conversation was interrupted by the return of the errant Sebastian Pimbleby.

"Your father told me that he left you in the care of a gentleman."

Sebastian looked into Catherine's eyes searchingly. Daniel noticed Catherine's mouth may have smiled at him, but the smile did not reach her eyes. Instead of twinkling, they now looked dull and soulless.

"Now, I wonder what you could be discussing with a renowned man like Professor Leicester?"

He smiled up at Daniel. Catherine donned another forced smile to compensate for her humiliation and her fiancé's rudeness.

"Sebastian, where are your manners? Professor Leicester is one of my father's closest professional associates."

"Hush now, Catherine. Don't lecture me.
Daniel here is the lecturer."

Catherine ignored his snide comment. Sebastian extended his limp and clammy hand to the professor, who shook it with a firm manly grip. Daniel formed an instant and accurate opinion of Sebastian. *This nasty little man is nothing more than a selfish bully.*

Sir Sebastian Pimbleby, just shy of twenty-eight years of age, was a stocky little man with a square face reminiscent of a bulldog. His meaty shoulders strained the sleeves of his dandy dinner jacket, and his tight fashionable trousers did not suit his short, chunky legs. His hair was plastered down against his greasy scalp, and he was already displaying a florid appearance brought on by excessive drinking.

Catherine stood almost a head taller than her fiancé, and Daniel wondered what on earth such an elegant woman saw in the ugly little fellow.

"As a matter of fact, Catherine and I have been having a fascinating conversation. She has surprised me with her palaeontology knowledge and of the fossils discovered in this area," said Daniel with a smile, as he stretched the truth to breaking point.

Sebastian frowned at Catherine trying to force her to speak, but she remained quiet. His fiancée's social disobedience maddened him.

"I see," said Sebastian at last, tiring of trying to control her with his invisible strings of shame. "Perhaps, she may have learnt a little from her father after all."

Daniel nodded. Keen to change the subject, he asked:

"And what is your family's primary business?"

"We farm with pigs," answered Sebastian proudly.

Daniel patronised him with a fake smile.

"Well, I suppose somebody has to put the bacon on the table."

Sebastian recognised the slight but did not respond. Knowing the conversation would end in disaster, Catherine interrupted them nervously.

"Please excuse me, Professor Leicester, I see my brothers."

Now in silence, the three of them stood awkwardly. Catherine breathed in deeply through her nose. The air hissed as it rushed into her lungs, but Sebastian didn't pick up on the signal.

"Sebastian," she grizzled to her fiancé, "will you please escort me across the room?"

"Of course, my dear," he replied, too stupid to realise that Catherine was berating him.

As Daniel watched them walk away, he saw Sebastian take her arm and whisper something in her ear. He squeezed her by the shoulder, just a little squeeze at first, which seemed to get firmer, his chubby fingers clearly digging into the flesh of her upper arm. Only when she mouthed the words 'I am sorry,' did he relax his grip. Daniel noticed some red blotches began to appear on Catherine's arm. When she looked down and saw them, vigorously she rubbed the marks with the palm of her hand, hoping they would disappear.

Daniel could feel the anger rise in his chest. *I bet he treats his pigs better.* He began planning what he would do to Pimbleby if he found him alone in a dark place. The dinner gong saved Sebastian from further scrutiny, and the party moved towards the dining hall.

"I hope that Catherine wasn't a burden," Sir Frankland said to Daniel after dinner. "Please forgive her if she was petulant. She is so stubborn at times. Her mother and I don't know what to do with her."

"Nothing to forgive, Sir," said Daniel smoothly, "Your daughter is delightful."

Despite thinking back to the tongue-lashing, he had received when he questioned her choice of spouse, Daniel smiled. It was not the first time he had to lie to a doting parent.

"Did you meet that Pimbleby fellow?"

"Yes, I did."

"What do you make of him? She is insisting on marrying the fellow. I am heartbroken about it."

Daniel gave his friend a compassionate chuckle.

"I'm sorry, Herbert. I have no experience in matters of the heart."

"Yes, well, keep it that way, my man. Life is simpler without women."

"People are always advising me of that. Married men and fathers of daughters, usually," confessed Daniel with a grin.

To cope with the rigours of enforced socialising, Daniel sensed he had consumed far too much fine wine. He bobbed and weaved his way through the guests, keen to find his friend Javier. As he reached the threshold of the great hall, he saw Catherine and her mother, Lady Anna arguing in hushed tones. The only words he heard Catherine say were 'I won't!' Lady Anna shook her head as her daughter stormed off to her room.

Javier caught sight of a tipsy Daniel staring at Catherine Frankland as she ascended the broad staircase and decided to make his way over. Daniel clapped a large, heavy hand on his colleague's shoulder.

"Please stop me if I ever have thoughts of marrying that girl."

Javier laughed at him and his booze-loosened tongue.

"Daniel, no woman will win your heart—you will be a bachelor forever."

"I concurrr," slurred Daniel. "Goodnight, my friend."

Javier watched his pal teeter up the stairs, chuckling as he saw him turn left at the top of the landing, only to retrace his steps moments later, when he realised his room was off to the right.

The next morning, Daniel woke with a thumping headache. It felt like a hammer beating against his brain, and he had no idea how long he would have to endure the suffering. Usually, it was a full day of pain for something of this magnitude, but he hoped for better.

He lamented getting so hungover and then lay back against his pillows and remembered the night before. His mind settled on Catherine, and he laughed. She was as glamorous as she was difficult. *Why would a woman with her qualities would want to marry a lout like Pimbleby?* Catherine seemed feisty and independent, which for him at least, were not bad qualities in a woman. It troubled him when he remembered how Pimbleby savagely gripped her arm, but Daniel had an unwritten rule—never interfere in matters of the heart, especially other people's.

She was beautiful and young, and she had her whole life ahead of her. He recalled the large grey eyes and luscious curled lashes, and he sighed as he imagined the perfect curves under her evening dress. Picturing her naked aroused him, but he gave up all his fantasies of the beautiful Catherine as the worsening headache finally overwhelmed his brain. *Paying attention to someone rambling on about tedious fossils is going to be a challenge today. For several reasons.*

5

THE HORSE RIDE

Their second meeting that weekend was more memorable than the first, mainly, because Daniel noted that was the exact moment he fell in love with Catherine Frankland.

Daniel had slept in until midday. Opening his dry, scratchy eyes, the dull thud in his head and tiresome self-inflicted nausea reminded him of the party excesses the night before, he groaned. Although in desperate need of a glass of whisky, a hair of the dog to fix things, he couldn't bear the thought of circulating with the houseguests just yet. Instead, he opted for some fresh air to soothe him. He crept downstairs quietly called the butler aside.

"Mr Rogers, may I please use Sir Herbert's stables. I would love to explore the countryside."

"Of course, Sir. I will arrange it straight away," advised Rogers. "Would you like a gentler steed, Sir?" asked the butler.

"Whatever you can arrange will be fine, thank you," replied Daniel with confidence, aware of the needling he was receiving for being a mere city dweller.

Rogers escorted Daniel to the stables and asked the boys to select a suitable horse for Sir Herbert's guest.

It had rained heavily in the morning. The air was still and crisp, and the ground wet. In case it began to rain again, Daniel put on an oilskin cape. It was the first time in months that he'd had an opportunity to ride. With a deep breath, gazing off towards the horizon, he looked forward to the sense of freedom as he explored the magnificent countryside.

As soon as he mounted the beast, the powerful stallion reared. *Those wretched boys have given me the wildest horse in the stable!* Looking out from behind a door, the lads giggled as Daniel fought to get the horse out of the stable yard without losing his dignity. It was a struggle, and he breathed a sigh of relief when he made it into the field without falling off.

Puddles covered the ground. It was cold, but liberating, being alone outdoors. The horse climbed the path to the top of a grassy mound, which overlooked the rocky shoreline. Daniel could just make out the Frankland house, now a shadow in the grey landscape.

In the distance, he saw a lone rider approaching, trekking up the path towards him. He was on edge. Poachers were ever-present, and he was not in the mood for a mistaken confrontation on somebody else's land.

He waited patiently to see who it might be, but the rider was wearing a hood, their face and body concealed. He decided to descend and to meet the person halfway and offer a friendly greeting. As he got closer, he could see that it was a woman. The rocky path ahead was treacherous in places. Whoever it was had to be a confident rider and know the track well to avoid injuring their horse. When he saw that it was Catherine, he relaxed a little.

"Good afternoon, Lady Frankland," said Daniel heartily.

"Good afternoon, Professor. What a fine and bracing day it is!" she answered with a broad smile.

"I see that you are without your beloved fiancé again."

"And I noticed that you were a terrible house guest and absent at luncheon," she retaliated.

He nodded, staring at Catherine's great white stallion.

"A fine animal."

"Arabian."

"A gift?"

"Yes, from my father."

"From a local stud farm?"

"No, Sir, I chose him in Arabia myself. You are not the only person who has travelled the world, Professor Leicester."

He gave her an apologetic look to atone for his presumptuousness. She continued.

"He brought me across the empty quarter. We travelled from Abu Dhabi across the desert to Arabia, and that is where I found him. We also met up with Gertrude Bell. she was my inspiration."

"And you are choosing to marry that country bumpkin pig farmer," said Daniel with a smirk.

Her eyes flashed, and her temper flared.

"Why? Are you suggesting should I marry you instead?" she countered.

Daniel laughed.

"You should at least marry a man who can give you the exotic adventures you dream of.

It seems to me you have settled for something much less than that."

He watched her closely, relishing in his opportunity to tease her. She looked down, uncertain of herself. He felt a little guilty and softened.

"Let us take the long path back to the house," he suggested. "The fresh sea air will do us good."

She nodded in agreement but did not speak. She turned the horse around and began her return to the stables.

Catherine cantered ahead of him. She was a confident horsewoman, and she had complete control of the handsome animal. She sat upright in the saddle, and he watched her, dressed in jodhpurs and boots, a fit, strong modern woman. Her face was white from cold, and her long dark lashes contrasted with her skin. She had the body of a woman, warm and inviting, with full breasts and sensual curves.

When they reached the end of the winding path, he manoeuvred his horse next to her, and they rode side by side, their legs almost touching. Catherine eventually broke the silence.

"Why do you hate Sebastian Pimbleby?" she enquired.

"Do you really want me to confirm what you already know?"

"And what is that, pray tell?"

"You aren't in love with him, Catherine. It is a practical arrangement at best. If you were besotted with him, you wouldn't be out here alone, deep in thought."

"Is that so? I think you are rather presumptuous, Professor Leicester."

Daniel laughed loudly.

"You are impossible. What do you want me to tell you? Must I feign that I think he is a fine gentleman?"

"What do you mean?"

"Catherine, I watched Sebastian Pimbleby grab your arm last night, and there was nothing gentle in his gesture. Your skin looked like it would bruise from the force of his grasp."

"You don't know him like I know him," replied Catherine defensively.

"Take off that oilskin and roll up your sleeve. I want to see your arm. Prove me wrong, and I will concede."

She looked at him with annoyance.

"Come on, do it!" he ordered her. "I think we both know what we will see."

"No."

"Fine. Have it your way. Mark my words, Catherine, he is an arrogant bully, and he is going to hurt you."

They continued without speaking. He watched her strong and sporty hips bouncing in the saddle, and he wondered why she would surrender herself to a man like Pimbleby.

Against Daniel's better judgement, he began weighing up the possibilities of seducing the beautiful woman beside him. In a moment of madness, he reached across and took the reins of her horse, gently pulling the stallion toward him. He twisted in his saddle and reached out his other arm for Catherine. He put his hand around her neck, and tenderly pulled her mouth towards him. She gasped in fear.

Seizing the opportunity to kiss her, he did his trademark smouldering gaze. This time, however, it failed him. Angry, she tried to pull away, but Daniel held her firmly until he felt her respond.

"I want you," he said in his best deep and sensual tone.

Daniel was convinced that she would cooperate. Few women rejected him when he delivered his signature move. This time, however, he was wrong. Catherine's spurning of his advance took him by surprise.

> "Come to my room," he whispered. "I will love you. Treat you properly."
>
> "You are a monster!" She spat at him. "Never!"

He wiped the saliva from his face in shock. Catherine sat upright in the saddle and with a subtle dig of her heels, the horse leapt forward until it reached a full gallop. She drove the white Arabian harder still, even though it was thundering toward a sizeable dry-stone wall that separated the meadowland from the Frankland estate.

Daniel held his breath, convinced that they could not make the jump. At the last second, one and a half paces before the wall, the great white stallion launched into the air in the most graceful equestrian motion that Daniel had ever seen. Catherine and the horse cleared the wall with space to spare and landed effortlessly. She didn't look back. Her cape flapped wildly behind her as she disappeared over the horizon.

Professor Daniel Leicester shook his head in awe and smiled from ear to ear. Lady Catherine Rebecca Frankland was an incredible, if feisty, woman, and he knew in that instant, he was in love with her.

When he got back to the house, he scribbled a note and pushed it underneath Catherine's door. He wasn't good with words, so it merely asked her to meet him for tea in the drawing-room.

Catherine returned to her bedroom, with her mother two paces behind wanting to know everything about the ride. On seeing the letter, the young woman read it then tore it to shreds in a furious temper.

"Who sent you that?" asked her mother.

"Nobody important."

Anna picked up some of the pieces of paper and pieced them together, deciding from the untidy scrawl it was a man's handwriting.

"Catherine," asked her mother gently, "are you in love with somebody else?"

"Oh, mother, Not this again. I have chosen Sebastian. We have set a wedding date, and he loves me," she answered with a tired tone of pure contempt.

"I saw you talking to Professor Leicester last night."

"Yes, I was. It was father's idea. I do not like the fellow."

Now Catherine had all her mother's attention, she made her position clear.

"He is rude. He ignored me most of the time. And—he is— frightfully old."

> "He is a well-respected man! And thirty-five is not 'frightfully old'." Anna said in frustration. "Catherine, you need to choose an adequate suitor. Your father and I are not satisfied with your choice in the slightest. Heaven only knows what you have seen in Pimbleby. The wedding date is not yet set. The wedding banns have not been read. People will understand you acted in haste. It wouldn't be the first broken engagement. You have sufficient time to change your mind, fix this sorry mess— if you can stop being so stubborn."

Catherine looked at her with fury. Anna shook her helpless head in despair.

> "We have always preferred that you choose your partner rather than force you into a match. But I don't know how much further your father's patience can stretch."

Eventually, Anna gave up the conversation. For a good six months, she knew that Catherine was not in love with her fiancé, but the wayward girl was still intent on marrying Sir Sebastian Pimbleby, even if she went against her parents' wishes. They wondered if defying them was the only reason she had settled on him.

It was now Sunday morning, and the guests attended the nearby Protestant church in the village. Most of the academics were self-professed atheists, but in public, they kept up the pretence of belief.

It was years since Daniel was in a church. He was not enamoured by religion as a means to explain the world around him. He had witnessed how it had wreaked havoc and ruined lives. At Christmas, and only Christmas, he attended religious events. The carol singing and mulled wine made it more bearable. He preferred to contribute to the season of goodwill by funding the merrymaking for his fellow villagers, than piously praising the Lord.

Daniel arrived at the churchyard in good time and greeted people as they arrived. In his tailored suit, he looked well turned out for once. Everybody commented on his outfit being a change from his usual baggy tweed attire. The cold weather forced the gathering congregants into the church. As one of the first there, Daniel found himself sitting close to the altar. The uncomfortable old pew forced him to sit upright in the seat, and unintentionally, gave him a stately elegance. It also made him look interested in what was happening.

He looked around, taking in the sights and smells he had experienced as a child: the oak panels and seating, the smell of old books, the smoke from the tall candles.

Daniel never realised that falling in love could fill a man with such confusion. He was frustrated that it was taking such a lot of work just to meet Catherine for a spot of afternoon tea, let alone anything else. Her parents did not seem concerned about her roaming around without a chaperone. In fact, compared to a lot of girls her age, she acted most liberally. His romantic dream was kept alive, knowing that no one agreed with Catherine pinning her future happiness on Sebastian.

The confident professor felt his heart beat faster each time the church door squealed opened. *Is it her?* Finally, the Frankland family arrived en masse. Sir Herbert escorted his wife, Lady Anna, his four sons and daughter Catherine to the front of the church. The family took up the pew in front of Daniel and Javier.

"God will strike me dead for being in a Protestant church," lamented Javier.

"You have been in the tombs of pagans, Javier, and you are still here," grunted Daniel.

"You don't understand my Catholic wife's view on the matter, Daniel. This must never get out. Do you promise me?"

"Si, I promise," said Daniel, too preoccupied watching Catherine to pay proper attention to his friend.

"Not one word, my friend. My mother-in-law is like a modern embodiment of the Spanish Inquisition. She will tie me to the stake and cut off my—"

"Javier, for goodness sake, stop it! Your secret is safe with me," Daniel whispered, suppressing the urge to laugh out loud.

The Franklands were seated, and Daniel was delighted to be so close to her once more. That delight was replaced with irritation as Sebastian sidled up alongside her.

Catherine had seen Daniel as she took her seat. Her heart had fluttered in her chest at the sight of him, a feeling she fought hard to stifle. He nodded gently and smiled at her, but she didn't acknowledge him in the slightest. He felt invisible. Daniel did not hear one word of the service, nor did he follow one line of the liturgy. He held the bible in his hand and did not open it because his eyes were riveted on Catherine. Daniel studied the graceful curve of her neck, her perfect posture, her lush curly fair hair against her white skin. His thoughts began to wander onto more carnal matters, and he had to remind himself of where he was.

Daniel's mood soared when he heard the reverend utter his familiar closing words, 'Go in peace.' Leaving the church sounded an excellent idea and could not happen a moment too soon.

It was Lady Anna who saw him standing with Javier,

"Our other guests are leaving early. Since you are leaving tomorrow, please join us for dinner, Daniel. The entire family is together for the first time in months."

"Thank you, Lady Anna. I gladly accept."

Catherine had dodged being near Daniel, making herself as elusive as possible. The last glimpse he had of her was being escorted to her father's carriage by Sebastian.

Her mother decided not to tell Catherine there would be an extra dinner guest.

"Ah, Daniel, you have arrived. How wonderful to see you," announced Lady Anna Frankland.

Catherine had been facing the parlour fire, lost in thought. When she heard his name, she spun around and glared at her mother. Daniel nodded politely. He shook hands with all the men and gleefully accepted a large glass of brandy.

"How is your father's estate managing this winter, Daniel?" asked Sir Herbert.

"As you know, it has been a reasonably mild winter so far. We have healthy livestock, and I have enough reserves to feed the staff if they need help."

"I am glad to hear that, Daniel. It seems that your father has reliable tenants."

"Yes, he has. We are most fortunate."

"Come with me, sit at the fire, and we can continue the conversation there."

"Was this your idea?" Catherine hissed at her mother.

"No, Catherine, I simply invited him for a meal because your father and your brothers enjoy Daniel's company. This house does not centre around you," she replied, annoyed at Catherine's overreaction.

"All you need to do is behave like a lady. Show some manners towards our guest."

Dinner was strained with the family overcompensating for the apparent tension between Daniel and Catherine. She was either very rude with the choice of words she directed at him or ignored him completely. Her father gave her a stern look that he hoped she would understand to mean 'enough!'. His ploy worked.

For the rest of the evening, Catherine did not utter a word. She acted the perfect lady. Daniel knew the struggle required for her to contain her emotions. *I would much prefer to have Catherine as her usual feisty self, rather than this watered down, muted version sat in front of me.*

Daniel eventually got the opportunity to speak privately to her in a small annexe off the dining room. She had quietly retreated into the little place in the hope that nobody would miss her. But she could not escape the watchful gaze of Daniel. He looked around furtively, then followed her.

When she looked up, she saw him standing in the archway.

"Catherine," he said commandingly. "Look, I won't beat about the bush here. I want to marry you."

She shook her head.

"It's too late, Daniel. Sebastian is my betrothed. Please, can you just accept that and stop pestering me? Why does everyone think it is their business to tell me what to do?" she protested.

Reluctantly, Daniel seemed to accept her answer as final. Catherine saw his crestfallen look. *You'll never change her mind. This pursuit of her is doomed. Face facts.* She looked into his pained eyes, and to his dismay, his resolve melted again. It was like some invisible force had control of his tongue.

"If you change your mind—"

"—I won't!" she interrupted.

"—You know where to find me."

He turned on his heels and left her in the annexe, just as he had found her—alone. He bid goodnight to Herbert and Anna and retired for the evening.

In the early hours of the morning, he awoke from a restless slumber after hearing a faint knock at the door. He gently opened it and found Catherine stood there. This time, her warm and friendly expression seemed to imply camaraderie rather than preface yet another snide confrontation. Without saying a word, he pulled her into the room. As the door gently swung closed, he kissed her tenderly, then held her in his strong muscular arms.

She tried to say something, but he silenced her by resting this forefinger lightly on her moistened lips.

> "This is no time to talk, Catherine," he whispered as he tried to close in on her mouth again.

She pushed him away.

> "You have to listen to me, Daniel. This cannot go on. There can never be a future for us. Go back to London. Leave me alone."

> "Since when can you give me orders, Miss Frankland? Besides, it's you who came to see me just now."

> "I have my reasons for visiting."

He flopped down into one of the two big chairs by the fireplace.

"Come, sit here," he said, his hand tapping on the arm of the other Chesterfield. "What is going on in that strong-willed head of yours?"

Rather than take the other seat, hesitantly, she curled up on his lap and looked into his eyes, knowingly leading him on. There was something about them that told her she was safe. She knew that the attraction she felt to Daniel was nothing that she had experienced with another man. Sebastian Pimbleby didn't enter her thoughts as Daniel began to loosen the buttons of her nightshirt. Suddenly, she pulled herself away from him. *What is it this time? She blows so hot and cold.*

"I have to tell you something, Daniel."

"What is it?"

She blurted out her confession in one single sentence.

"I have slept with Sebastian Pimbleby. I am not a virgin."

"I must say I am confused. I don't see Pimbleby as someone you would freely choose to sleep with."

"Sebastian has threatened to disgrace me if I refuse to marry him. Nobody will ever take me for a wife. You know how high society works, Daniel, men can have their mistress and whores, but their wife must be virtuous."

Daniel let her continue. She was becoming more and more distressed, angry and resentful of the hypocrisy of Victorian society.

"My parents will be mortified if he announces it to the whole world that I am nothing more than a common harlot. My brothers, they hate him. It will cause a war between the Franklands and the Pimblebys. I am trapped."

"No. You might be afraid, but you are not trapped."

"It is one and the same."

"Your family will never discard you."

"The Franklands will be gossiped about around parliament, and I will bring shame to my father if this becomes common knowledge."

"Yours will not be a true marriage if it is based on coercion and fear, Catherine. Rest assured, some men fall in love, get married and love their wives passionately. Those men don't question their wife's past."

"Are you—one of those men?" she whispered

"Yes, I am."

He kissed her gently and slid his hand under the neckline of her robe and touched her bosom. He looked into her eyes as he felt her warm, rounded body. In a single, smooth movement, he picked her up and carried her to the bed. He removed his shirt and then his trousers as she looked on. He lay next to her stroking her skin. She was more beautiful than he had imagined. It took all his resolve not to go any further. He took that pleasure in his mind alone.

She woke up in his arms, barely an hour before breakfast. She realised where she was and smiled. He had not slept at all but stayed awake watching her and building a future for them in his mind. She was passionate and fearless and would travel the world with him. Then they would settle and have children. The family would have great adventures and reminisce about them when they were old. He would never let her go. He would love her forever.

Catherine glanced at the carriage clock on the dresser.

"I have to go now, else we risk getting caught," she lamented.

"Not just yet," Daniel whispered.

He looked into her eyes and kissed her.

"I have to marry him."

"He won't love you like I love you," he urged earnestly.

"I know, Daniel—but I have my reasons."

He kissed her goodbye, and as soon as she left, he wanted her back.

6

THE RELUCTANT BRIDE

Catherine Frankland and Sebastian Pimbleby were married in the autumn. The fallen leaves around the church were a lush carpet of red, orange and yellow. The bride's snow-white dress shone in the weak morning sunlight, giving the impression that an angel was entering the country churchyard.

She walked through the grand arched doors, and she saw the groom waiting for her. Her father gently wiped the tears from her beautiful face.

"It's not too late to turn back, Catherine," Sir Herbert said to her. "I don't give a damn what anybody says, just your happiness."

"No, Father. I can only go forward now."

"Catherine, my child, I am prepared to risk everything for you," he said with a voice cracking with emotion.

"I know, Papa, but you don't need to."

Lady Anna watched her daughter, and she remembered the love she had felt for her husband on their wedding day, and she knew that the tears Catherine was shedding were not of joy, but remorse.

Halfway down the aisle, Catherine remembered Daniel's words, *'He won't love you like I love you.'* She had to muster all her self-control to not sob her heart out.

She stood before the altar, and she saw the pig farmer for what exactly he was—a bully who wanted to use her as a step up in society. Glancing at his smug, selfish face sickened her. The idea that he would be allowed to touch her for the rest of her life filled Catherine with horror. Still, she was brave, much braver than Daniel could ever understand. She was marrying the brute she hated for everybody else, to be seen to conform, committing to a lonely, loveless future purely to protect her family name.

Sebastian Pimbleby took her his new wife a tour of Italy, and at least Catherine was able to fall in love with something on her honeymoon—the sun-drenched countryside. The simple airy Tuscan houses, devoid of clutter, appealed to her sense of space and freedom. When they went to Naples, she was charmed by the joy and zest displayed by ordinary people going about their daily work. Their final destination was the Isle of Capri in the Gulf of Naples. Catherine sat on the balcony, looking at the azure ocean. She wanted to hire a guide and go to the Blue Grotto, but Sebastian would not hear of it.

> "It's too blasted hot!" he moaned as big beads of sweat formed on his fat forehead. "Besides, it is far too unladylike to have you clambering over rocks like a navvy in a railway cutting. And what if you should fall, then what?" he chided.

Catherine felt like a caged animal as she desperately tried to contain her temper. She let her mind wander to better things. The first thing it encountered was a vision of Daniel. *He would have no qualms about the grotto, and we would have swum in the blue water every day.* She thought of the life of adventure she could have had with him. Compared him to Pimbleby, an uptight class-conscious bore, enamoured by everything British, Daniel was a true cosmopolitan delight.

Her pleasant reverie was broken by more of Sebastian's piercing whining.

> "I cannot understand how people can like this place," he complained. "The people are vulgar. The food is dreadful. The heat is unbearable. I cannot wait to get back to England."

Catherine dreaded the thought of going home with him and being subject to the boredom that accompanied the dark nights.

On the last leg of the journey home, their ship sailed into a tempestuous storm just outside Southampton. Every time the bow of the boat plunged into the crashing waves, the huge hull shuddered and creaked against the iron-hard sea. Torrents of water flooded the deck. It sloshed from side to side as the ship which leaned and groaned in the violent weather. For twelve awful hours, the captain made the decision to moor up just outside the port. In those extreme conditions, trying to reach for land was simply too dangerous. Anchoring up was the lesser of two evils.

Catherine was stuck with her husband, who insisted on making love to her on the tossing ship. Thankfully, the events transpired quickly, but his brief panting and writhing disgusted her. She did her best to get lost in her thoughts.

She recalled her first time with Sebastian—the episode that had begun her downfall. It was at a party held on the Pimbleby Estate. Sebastian had followed her throughout the evening, like a besotted puppy. He finally approached her, and an uncomfortable conversation ensued. It was a shallow exchange of pleasantries, and eventually, she excused herself from his tiresome company.

Sebastian Pimbleby learnt his deep disrespect for women from his father, Sir Edward. He had great admiration for the man, mainly because of his cruel streak. 'A woman must know her place,' his father used to say.

On the day of his sixteenth birthday, Sebastian's father paid for his favourite prostitute to introduce his boy to the manly pleasures of physical love. She came highly experienced in carnal matters, but to survive her tough career, her skills deliberately excluded any form of emotion, tenderness or affection. That set the tone for Sebastian, who duly applied these callous mechanical methods to all his romantic encounters.

Surreptitiously, Sebastian ignored her implied request to leave her alone at the party and followed Catherine everywhere, stalking her like a deer. Eventually, he watched her go outside onto the veranda for some fresh air and followed her.

"Are you enjoying yourself, Catherine?" he asked, trying to touch her hand.

"Yes, thank you," she answered politely.

"I am glad that I found you unaccompanied."

"I think it is best we are not seen alone together, Sebastian. Tongues will wag," she said, needing an excuse to go back inside.

"But your beauty has led me here, Catherine."

She felt uncomfortable with this show of empty flattery, but felt she could not be impolite to her host. She looked around frantically for her father or her brothers, but they were nowhere to be seen.

"My father says it is time I found myself a wife."

He took a step nearer, and his close proximity made her flinch. She took a few steps back towards the far corner of the flagstones. This would prove to be a terrible decision.

"I think that you can make me happy, Catherine."

"I have not yet decided whom I wish to marry."

She answered with a kind but firm tone in her voice, hoping that would put an end to the matter.

"Well, let me decide for you," he said, smiling with malice.

Knowing none of the houseguests could see the far corner of the veranda through the slender ballroom windows, he grabbed her roughly by her arm and dragged her down the stone steps into the garden. At first, stunned at the turn of events, she did not know whether to cry for help and be socially humiliated or to physically fight him off.

With a deep breath, she decided to fight and slapped him across his face, but he undeterred, remaining strong and aggressive. Feeling even angrier and entitled, he ignored her flurry of punches signalling for him to stop. Roughly, Sebastian shoved Catherine onto the ground. He roughly clapped his chubby hand over her mouth. Her face stung.

"If you scream again, I will hurt you more than I intend to, you arrogant wench."

Catherine strained to see the house, but it was useless. Her location was concealed by thick rhododendron bushes. Inside, the small string quartet was playing, and the guests were talking and laughing loudly over the music. So far from the house, nobody could see or hear her.

Sebastian unbuttoned his trousers and savagely pulled up her dress. She felt wet grass and mud on her bare legs. He fell with his full weight on top of her. She struggled to breathe. Sebastian took no chances and covered her mouth once more while he pushed himself inside her. It was all over in four thrusts. She started crying. She was cold and dirty, and felt her crumpled up dress soaking up Sebastian's warm stain.

"There, Catherine," he whispered in her ear. "I have made up your mind for you. You will be my bride. And if you don't marry me, I will spread the rumour that you wanted me to deflower you, begged me. They know you are wild of heart, delighting in going against what society expects. Everyone knows that it is a sign of loose morals in a woman. No eligible bachelor in England will want second-hand goods. You and your family will be scandalised."

"No! It is your word against mine."

"I'm afraid not," said Sebastian.

She looked at him dazed, too traumatised to understand why he felt he would have the upper hand. Things soon became clear. Sebastian signalled for his two thuggish brothers to step out of the shadows. Sir Edward made sure all of the Pimbleby boys became ruthless misogynists. They looked down at her with pure scorn, pointing and sniggering at her nakedness from the waist down.

"She practically begged you, Sebastian!" said the elder brother as the younger one laughed at her contemptuously.

Sebastian gave the two men a proud grin then looked down at her.

"If this gets out, you are ruined, Catherine. You are a fallen woman. There are no choices now. Therefore, I will ask one more time—do you accept my proposal?"

She was too frightened to answer. Sebastian grabbed her by her hair and pulled her to her feet as the two henchmen brothers looked on.

> "I trust you now accept my proposal, dearest Catherine?" Sebastian demanded, shaking her roughly with each syllable, her head and limbs lolling about like a lifeless rag doll's.

Knowing things would only get worse if she did not comply, Catherine regained her composure and nodded her 'agreement'.

> "Now go and clean yourself up! Get that mud off your dress. We can't make the announcement with you looking so terrible. I want you back in the ballroom within fifteen minutes."

As she sneaked back towards the house under cover of darkness, she could hear Sebastian's brothers slapping him on the back and congratulating him on his forthcoming nuptials. Furiously, she brushed at her dress as the mud dried and hoped the dirty marks would be lost in the pattern. She felt the psychological mark Sebastian had left upon her would never disappear.

A short while later, Sebastian announced their engagement to the delighted guests while Catherine stood next to him, biting her lip to fight back the tears. It took all of her gutsy resolve to put on a brave face in public. Her parents were furious at the news, her brothers murderous. They all detested the uncouth ruffian that was Sebastian Pimbleby. They were surprised their low opinion of him had managed to sink lower still. By not asking Sir Herbert for his daughter's hand in marriage first, he had disobeyed all social protocol. For the Frankland family, Catherine had a lot of explaining to do for agreeing there and then rather than deferring her decision.

When she thought of that night, she felt disgust for Sebastian and disgust for herself. Hindsight it seemed was a wonderful friend who always arrived a little too late to assist. She should have fought harder and screamed louder. Why didn't she call her mother aside and tell Anna what he had done? Everyone knew Sebastian was a horrible man, and that persuading good people that he was lying about the encounter was not beyond the realms of possibility. She tried to reason that he had terrified her, but that meant that she was weak—and for a strong, spirited woman like Catherine, she hated feeling weak.

Being on the ship with Pimbleby with nowhere to escape to was a nightmare. It was like being back in the garden bushes, except now Sebastian could legally assault her as often as he wished. Catherine tried to seek refuge in the memory of Daniel, imagine he was on top of her, but it was futile. Cruel and crass Sebastian was nothing like the calm and considerate professor. No amount of imagining or mental distraction would bridge the gap.

> "I intend to take you home pregnant, Catherine. Nothing will please my parents more than knowing that I have sired an heir."

Catherine knew that the purpose of the aristocratic woman was to breed noble children by the half-dozen. In her naivety, she had not considered that it could happen so soon. Of all the duties as a wife, the thought of birthing one child after the next, with the inherent mortal risk that entailed, was the one thing appalled her the most about her future. She found it very difficult to look cheerful about the idea, and eventually, Sebastian lost his temper.

In their cabin, he stood in front of her, naked, every bit of his body pink and freckled. He erupted into an epic rage. As he pushed her head down, the soft inside of her cheek was crushed against her molars. The metallic taste of blood flooded her mouth. The ship rose on a wave and fell violently into the trough. After hours of the ship's pitch and yaw, Catherine could not help herself as her nausea rose up. She heaved and was sick all over Sebastian. He screamed in disgust. Many years later she and Janey would look back, and their shared black humour would see the funny side of it, but at the time, Catherine was terrified.

After six months of daily abuse, Catherine felt she could not continue in the marriage. Worse, Sebastian was a regular patron of a brothel in the next county which made her despair all the more. The last thing she wanted was a bout of syphilis to add to her woes.

When he was with her, Sebastian was a heavy-handed drunk. She sought the counsel of her mother-in-law. She thought since her own parents were lucky enough to marry for love as well as social advancement, perhaps the woman who had endured Sir Edward Pimbleby for decades could give her some advice on how to cope. It would be a delicate discussion, but Catherine felt she had no other choice if she were to endure being Sebastian's wife for much longer.

"Good afternoon, Catherine," said Lady Pimbleby, as she potted an orchid in the conservatory.

"Good afternoon," she responded cheerfully.

She smiled at her mother-in-law, hoping that it would soften the older woman's heart. That hope was doomed. Lady Pimbleby looked at Catherine, a truly modern woman, dressed in her jodhpurs and riding boots. As an older aristocratic lady with traditional views deeply rooted in the past, she would not have been seen in public in such inappropriate attire.

"Did you ride here?"

"Yes, my lady. It is a delightful day."

"I received your note, Catherine, and I am glad that you have come to visit me, my dear."

She stared at Catherine, proud that her son had secured such a beautiful wife. Catherine's fair hair was pinned up into a neat bun in the nape of her neck. Her face was flushed from the ride, and her pink cheeks gave her a healthy glow.

They sat down at a small table in the corner of the conservatory to take afternoon tea. Before the refreshments arrived, they engaged in polite small talk.

For the new bride, the need to broach the subject of Sebastian's conduct burned hotter by the minute. After months of despair, eventually, Catherine could hold her tongue no longer.

"My lady, I have come here to seek your advice."

Lady Pimbleby's face lit up, and she smiled. She was almost sure that Catherine was going to confide her pregnancy. *At last, after six months, it seems my daughter-in-law has finally conceived. I will delight in being a grandmother. And if it is a boy, Edward will be delighted too— the estate will finally have an heir.*

"It is Sebastian," revealed Catherine.

"Is Sebastian ill?" asked his mother, concerned.

"No, my lady, he is well."

"Then what is the matter, Catherine?"

"Ma'am, I am here to beg you and Sir Edward to intervene. Sebastian has been visiting a—"

she stammered "—a business of ill repute in the next county."

The older woman's eyes turned as hard as steel.

"How dare you imply that my son would do anything of the sort?"

"My lady, I would not lie to you."

"Catherine, you are a young inexperienced woman. I can only imagine that this is either your imagination or that you do not please him sufficiently."

A dismayed Catherine sensed the conversation was not going to go the way she had hoped.

"You see, my dear, you have to remember—hmm. Perhaps your mother did not teach you this. You see, your husband's flesh must be satisfied properly if you want a peaceful marriage. I suggest that you go home and perform your wifely duties adequately."

Catherine felt demeaned. She did not know what had possessed her to ask her mother-in-law for help. She had hoped that Lady Pimbleby would offer a sympathetic ear and support her position. Her response made her seem more of an enemy than a supporter.

"By the way, Catherine, are there any signs that you may be with child?"

"No, my lady. Not yet."

"Have you considered that your husband is frustrated by your struggle to conceive?"

Catherine nodded, even though she knew that was not the root cause of Sebastian's brothel habit.

"Perhaps a visit to Harley Street may assist you."

"Yes. What an excellent suggestion. Thank you for your guidance in this matter," Catherine lied. "I have to go, my lady, I have an appointment."

"As you wish."

Catherine bid the old woman farewell and left the dismal Pimbleby family home mortified.

Distraught, she rode home as fast as she could. She and her horse were drenched in perspiration when she arrived at the guest cottage on the estate. From the outside, it looked enchanting, a twee little home, but for Catherine, it was a prison.

She ordered her bathtub to be filled and then poured herself a large glass of sherry which she drank in one gulp before pouring another. Finally, when the bath was ready, she stepped into the tub, lay back and let the soothing warm water wash over her. The sherry began to relax her mood, and she felt less emotional about her visit to her mother-in-law. *Perhaps the woman was right. Maybe if I were more subservient, the situation might change.*

She got out of the bath and dried herself off. By now, it was almost dinnertime, and she needed to take care of her appearance. Her hair was held back with two gold combs that her father had brought back from Japan. They were lacquered with delicate leaves and flowers. The vibrant colours contrasted with her fair hair. She put on a daring peacock blue dress which revealed her ivory shoulders. That night she was happy to suffer the cold to please Sebastian.

She had prepared a tray with his favourite wine and a cheeseboard, and set the cosy dining room table for two. Catherine took the trouble to decorate it with the most beautiful trimmings, filling the vases with bright cerise orchids from the conservatory.

Sebastian arrived in the dining room promptly at seven o'clock. He had not dressed for dinner. He looked dishevelled as he strode toward her with purpose. Catherine stood up to receive him in her elegant gown.

"Good evening, my darling," she greeted with a smile.

Sebastian didn't acknowledge her. Instead, he hit her across the face with a flat hand. She tumbled to the floor and could feel the burning sting of the slap. She was too shocked to cry, filled with terror that he may hit her again. He bent over, grabbed her hair and pulled her to her feet.

> "What the hell did you think you were doing speaking to my mother about our marriage?" he screamed, bending over so his mouth was almost pressed against her ear.

> "I—I needed help," she stuttered.

> "You needed help? What for?"

She didn't answer him, and he shook her violently.

> "I want a divorce," she said softly.

He hit her again, but harder. Her mouth began to bleed, and she felt her face start to swell.

> "If you ever leave me, I will hunt you down and kill you."

He yanked her to her feet.

> "Do I make myself clear?" he roared, immersing her in his alcoholic breath and spittle.

She nodded.

> "Say it!" he screamed.

> "Yes. I understand," she surrendered.

7

TRAPPED

In his luxurious oak-panelled office, the barrister looked at the beautiful young woman seated in front of him.

"So, am I correct in saying that you are seeking to divorce Sebastian Pimbleby?"

"Yes, Sir."

"As you know, it will be complicated to divorce your husband. Considering his status, it may be discussed in parliament?"

"Yes. I am aware of the consequences." Catherine said.

"It is also costly."

"Mr Richards, rest assured no price would be too high for me to be free of the man. Sebastian regularly frequents brothels. He beats me whenever the mood takes him. He treats me with constant cruelty, I simply cannot live under these conditions anymore."

"Can you supply proof of these accusations?"

"Proof?" she asked, annoyed that she had no bruising to show him that day.

"Witnesses, of course. Has anybody seen him in this brothel?"

"Nobody that will admit it, Sir, but the information has reached me."

"That is hearsay, Lady Catherine. In the courts, we work on hard facts, not gossip."

She shook her head in dismay,

"And what about the brutality, Mr Richards?"

"Again, if nobody has witnessed this behaviour, we have no case against him," advised the barrister.

"Do you have any children? You are aware that you will have to leave them with your husband and waive your access to them?" he continued.

"We do not have children, yet," confirmed Catherine relieved that there was perhaps one advantage to the whole sorry mess.

"Lady Catherine, do you realise that you will receive no money if you decide to leave your husband. And the chances of remarrying, well, they are slim to non-existent?"

"I do not want money from my husband, and I have no desire ever to marry again."

"Life will be a terrible struggle if you choose to divorce. Have you consulted your family regarding your decision?" he continued. "This unusual course of action will destroy the Franklands' reputation. I know that your father is a renowned academic. Do you realise that it will damage his career and probably ruin his future?"

Catherine gave Mr Richards her most determined look.

"If you were my daughter, I would advise you to return to your husband. Learn to manage the relationship to the best of your ability. Marriage is not easy, my dear. Unfortunately, it is not a typical contract. It is bounded by law until death."

Catherine left the office and burst into tears. There was no escape. No matter how her hard life became, she dared not take her family down with her in a bid to be rid of her husband. Yet, in her heart of hearts, she knew that no woman deserved the treatment that she was receiving. She had seen Sebastian treat his gun dog on a hunt better than her.

She was warned against Sebastian so many times, why had she been too scared to confide in her mother. *Why didn't I leave with Daniel?* The thought of Daniel depressed her even more. His words still echoed in her ears—'He will not love you like I love you.'

After the visit to Mr Richards, Catherine spent two weeks in torment. The more she deliberated, the more she was convinced that the only answer was to leave Hampshire and never return. She wouldn't be the first woman to run away. *I shall leave a letter for my parents telling them not to worry then I shall find a place where it was safe to live without the fear of Sebastian finding me. With the few bits of jewellery, I have, I can raise a little cash to tide me over. I shall rebuild my life again, one step at a time.*

Recently, in his latest drunken rage, Sebastian had threatened to kill her, and she knew that in a furious temper, he was capable of it. Rage would divert what was left of his moral compass to a murderous route. Lately, with her failure to conceive, he was becoming more irritable, more controlling. After the secret visit to her mother-in-law, Catherine now had to account for every minute of her day.

Her once full life with her parents had been whittled down to long days of isolation and the soul-sapping behaviour of pretending she loved him when it was the opposite.

> "Do you love me, Catherine?" he would shout in her face.

> "Of course, I do my darling," she would lie affectionately.

> "Oh, come on! I know you are lying. You don't, and you never did. Right from the first moment I lay with you, you have been plotting your escape. Except you were too stupid and powerless to manage it. I should get rid of you right now and find a woman who wants me."

She watched him in terror.

> "Don't look at me like that," he thundered, "And don't even think of leaving me. My brothers and I will seek terrible revenge on your parents and brothers."

The threats went on and on and on.

Eventually, she gave up trying to convince him that she cared. Each time he stood over her yelling abuse, all Catherine could do was pray that she would be able to stay alive long enough to escape.

When Sebastian left for the brothel after another brutal attack, she sat at her writing desk. *He will be gone until the morning with any luck. I must seize the day.* Despite the terrifying risk and the hardship that lay ahead of her, she made the difficult decision to flee. After writing and rewriting the difficult letter several times in her mind, eventually, she kept her message short and simple.

> *Dearest Papa and Mama,*
>
> *I will be going away for a short while. Please do not worry about me.*
>
> *I do not wish to go into detail but trust me when I say I cannot live with Sebastian any longer.*
>
> *No matter what, remember that I love you both.*
>
> *I will send you a letter when I reach my destination.*
>
> *Please do not tell Sebastian that I have contacted you.*
>
> *Your loving daughter,*
>
> *Catherine*

She carefully folded up the finished note and hid it up her sleeve. Then she carefully collected up her previous crumpled attempts and tossed them into the fire. Watching the writing paper burn to ash, taking her despair with it, was strangely cathartic.

The next morning was cold, far too cold to be out on horseback. Sadly, once again, Catherine found herself dealing with limited options. She dressed as warmly as she could and mounted her beautiful Arabian horse and rode out into the howling gale and horizontal rain.

She rode to the closest village and dropped the letter into the post box, trying not to cry. Her next task was to hurry along to a small railway siding that served as the local station and book herself a ticket on the late train to London. She placed the ticket in her saddlebag and then returned home to pack a small bag of clothes. She needed to leave most of her belongings behind to hide her escape bid. The few valuable possessions she had were already hidden near the stables, ready for her flight from her hateful husband.

Sebastian arrived home after dinner at the family home, drunk and aggressive.

> "Somebody saw you at the post office in the village," he said in a low, ominous voice.

She replied, feigning cheerfulness once again.

> "Oh, yes, I posted a letter to my parents. I have not written for some time. It is my father's birthday soon, and I wondered if they had any plans to celebrate."

> "You could have sent one of the servants," he countered.

"I felt like a ride, so I decided to take it myself."

"Perhaps the letter was for someone else, and not your father at all?" he asked, raising an eyebrow.

"No, Sebastian, truly. It was just a lovely day to ride."

"Don't you dare lie to me. The weather this morning was foul for the horse and rider. I see your oilskin jacket is resting on another peg. To go out in those conditions, well I can only assume it must have been a critical letter. What could be so critical, I wonder? Would you care to explain?"

"Please stop, Sebastian," she begged, exhausted from more of his threats and arguing.

"You will not leave this home, Catherine, do you hear? If I can't have you, no one will."

"It is wrong to lock me up like some sort of animal forever!" she screamed.

She expected him to slap her for her backchat, but he didn't. Instead, he left the room, slamming the door behind him.

Left alone in the now quiet room, a panicked yet relieved Catherine heard the blood pulse in her ears and her heart knock against her ribs.

The silence was punctuated suddenly by a rifle shot. Worryingly, it came from close by. She could not fathom who would be shooting so close to the house at this time of the night.

She heard footsteps running up the path and anxious knocking at the door.

> "My Lady, come quickly, come quickly, the master is in the stable," said the trembling maid.

Catherine ran to investigate, thinking, hoping, that Sebastian had harmed himself.

> "What has happened?" she cried as she reached the stables. "Where is Sebastian?"
>
> "He has left in the cab, Ma'am," said the stable hand. Catherine breathed a sigh of relief.
>
> "But I heard a gunshot, William? You can't have missed it, surely?"

William could not help himself as his eyes welled up with tears.

She instinctively knew what Sebastian had done. She pushed past William, who did his best to stop her but was thwarted in his efforts. A determined Catherine ran into the stable and looked over the Arabian's door. The poor animal lay on the straw, eyes wide open, with a bullet hole through its forehead, blood oozing from the wound.

Catherine became hysterical. She fell to her knees in front of the beast, put her head against his neck and sobbed. Every bit of pain she had experienced for the last few months crashed down upon her. *It seems my life cannot get any worse.* William pulled her away from the horse.

> "You have to get away from here, ma'am. If he comes back, who knows what else he will do. I don't want to speak out of turn, ma'am, but we have heard some things going on in the house between you and the master, and we are worried."

Catherine knew she would have to pull herself together if she wanted to survive the night. Sebastian was clearly unstable and acting like a mad man.

She told William to collect her bag as she dressed warmly in the oilskin once more covering her head with a thick woollen shawl.

> "I need to reach the station by ten o'clock," she muttered.

"There will be nobody on the old road at this hour, ma'am. It will take you just behind the sidings. Be careful."

"Thank you, William. Please don't tell him anything," she begged.

"Of course not. Go now. Oh, and ma'am—good luck."

8

FAILED PLANS

Sir Rufus Hamilton-Gordon sat in front of the fireplace at his private club, an island of peace in his ever-complex world. Sat alone, he relished the tranquil atmosphere. Rufus naturally qualified for membership because of his father's title and pedigree.

The large leather chair dwarfed the spindly man. As always, he dressed finely. Resting his elbow on the arm of the chair, he held his hand aloft. In it, was the most exceptional Cuban cigar that he could afford. His thin legs were crossed at the ankle in a most effeminate way.

His moment of solitude was interrupted when Sir Godfrey Roxbury landed in the chair opposite. Rufus looked at him and sighed inwardly, preparing himself for an uncomfortable conversation peppered with Roxbury's probing questions and his tiresome excuses.

"Rufus," he greeted in a refined voice.

"Oh, hello, Godfrey, old chap," said Rufus feigning cheeriness.

"How was your weekend at the Leicesters'? Agreeable, I trust?"

"Fine, Godfrey. Fine."

"Is there anything positive to report?"

"Of course, Godfrey. What do you take me for? Things progressed just as we planned."

"Really? So, old James Leicester agrees that we can form a cartel for arms manufacture."

"Godfrey, he positively jumped at the idea. I have never seen him this enthusiastic before. My secretary has delivered all the necessary documentation to the Ministry of Foreign Affairs. Now, the tendering process is a mere formality. We have been promised the contract."

"So, it is finalised then?"

"Yes. Our intelligence services have reported that without armed intervention, the situation will spiral into an international crisis. Thank God, Britain is there to manage the whole mess. I mean who else could, Godfrey?"

"Precisely, old boy. And the other matter, Rufus, the proposed marriage alliance between you and the Leicester family?"

"Oh that, yes," smiled Rufus wryly. "Well, of course, I see no problem going forward. We just need to get the formalities behind us."

"I hear that young Daniel Leicester is something of a wildcard?"

"I found him to be most agreeable, Godfrey," lied Rufus. "Of course, he has a lot to gain—a large fortune and the perfect society wife."

Sir Rufus made his way home in his carriage even though his home was very close to the club. His mind was burdened. Everything he had told Sir Godfrey Roxbury was a lie. He had no control over Sir James Leicester's actions whatsoever. Daniel was uncooperative at best.

If he were honest, the weekend at the Leicester estate had been disastrous. Although James liked the idea of the business merger, the man seemed to have no control over his son whatsoever. It was clear Daniel Leicester did not care for the trappings of society life, money or titles. *No, I am going to need another bargaining chip to reel in Daniel.*

Rufus had toyed with the idea of stifling his academic career. He quickly gave up the idea after realising Daniel was already a respected published scientist. If he tried to make his professional life miserable, far away Harvard or Yale would snap him up in an instant. Realistically, the only person who could salvage Sir Rufus' scheme was Dianna, and he planned to discuss it with her in the morning.

The beautiful Dianna sat in the breakfast room, drinking a cup of tea while she waited impatiently for her father to arrive. She was a spoilt only child. Rufus had watched his wife die as she gave his daughter life. Of course, he would have preferred a son, but that was not to be. These days, his daughter was the apple of his eye.

Dianna's genes were modelled on those of her father. She was slight of stature and could pass as a sixteen-year-old. Dianna had also inherited her father's lack of scruples. He was mercenary, conniving, creative and devious, skills which helped him successfully negotiate the treacherous pitfalls of politics.

"Good morning, Dianna," rang out the cheerful voice.

"Father," said Dianna without emotion.

"Did you rest well, my darling?"

"Yes, thank you."

"Excellent news. It's good you are feeling refreshed. We have a lot of work to do today."

She raised one perfect eyebrow and looked at him.

"Yes, I saw Sir Godfrey Roxbury last night. He is delighted with our progress."

"Progress?" asked Dianna, tilting her head to one side.

"Yes, he is delighted that we had such a successful weekend at the Leicesters."

Now he had broached the subject of the Leicesters he swiftly segued the discussion onto Daniel.

"Dianna, did your meeting with Daniel Leicester develop as we planned?"

"Of course, father."

"You did remember how important this union is?"

"Of course, father. I followed your instructions to the letter."

"Was he satisfied with your, mmm—" Rufus searched for the correct word. "—talents?"

"I am sure he was, father."

"Did the discussion touch on the subject of marriage?"

"Yes father, but didn't give the response you were hoping for. In very forthright terms, he told me our marriage was out of the question.

He said no one could tell him who he would marry—if he even chose to marry at all."

"So, your feminine methods of persuasion were not successful?" Rufus snarled.

"I did my best, father. I cannot do more than I have done."

"You stupid girl, have you learned nothing? Of course, there is more that you can do, Dianna." He jabbed his pointed finger at her with each syllable. "Now, you simply have to tell Daniel Leicester that you are pregnant."

"But I am probably not pregnant, father. How can we possibly get away with that explanation?"

"We will concern ourselves with the practical details later, Dianna. For now, it is the only solution to this problem."

"Father, you don't seem to understand. Daniel Leicester is not like other men. He cares not for what society expects of him. I doubt that he will consider marrying me even under those circumstances."

"No man wants his son raised a bastard, Dianna. If he had a child with some peasant girl in the country, he could hide it away and forget about it. But in our circle, he would never get away with it. He and his family will be disgraced."

"He doesn't care, father. Besides, he is away on digs a lot of the time. People will soon forget him when he is overseas. The shame will soon fade."

"Trust me, Dianna, he will care. Maybe not for you or society, but he will care for his child's future, especially if it is a boy. Daniel Leicester is a man of principle at heart, and as much as it annoys us, we have but one chance to use his ethics to our advantage. I think you know what is required."

Rufus stomped out of the breakfast room, furious. He had placed all his hopes on Dianna at the weekend, and she had failed him. The pregnancy, real or phantom, was the last chance he had to force Daniel's hand. *And it will be forced.*

Dianna lay on her bed deep in thought, plotting her actions. A marriage to Daniel Leicester would make her one of the most wealthy and powerful women in England. She knew that Daniel would never fall in love with her, but that mattered not compared with the boost in status and privilege. Plenty of society marriages were hollow shams of convenience for the families.

A seed of an idea began to germinate. She decided her close friendship with Daniel's sister Elizabeth could be exploited. *Yes, I shall let it slip to Elizabeth that I am expecting Daniel's child. She is such a blabbermouth she will surely tell Lady Leicester. But I shall visit Daniel first. I'd best not make an appointment too soon—leave it a month or so. That will be a reasonable amount of time to diagnose a pregnancy.* A selfish smirk formed on Dianna's face.

Back in Mayfair, Professor Daniel Leicester had a headache, and it was induced by stress. The trigger was Lady Catherine Rebecca Frankland appearing at his front door in the guise of a world-weary housekeeper, Miss Carter. Of everything he had dreamed of—and he had dreamed of her for three years—the last thing he expected was the beautiful love of his life looking at him from the door of his study, a person who was also his newly employed charwoman.

How am I going to survive the temptation of having her in my home without my feelings showing? She has to go. She spurned me for another man, an odious man at that. She cannot be trusted not to break my heart a second time. No matter how hard he tried, he could not relax. Eventually, he set out to find Javier.

"Señor Daniel, what a pleasant surprise! Come in! Gosh, you look tired."

Javier's unexpected guest nodded slowly in confirmation.

"Here's an idea, my friend. I am going on holiday to the continent soon. The rest will do you good. Come with me and meet my beautiful sisters."

Javier, grinning, made an hourglass wiggle with his hands.

"Sun. Sea. Señoritas!" he added with a wink.

Daniel frowned.

"That is what I have come to discuss—Señoritas."

"Aha, so you are joining me at last in Spain!" said the elated Javier.

"No, I can't."

"You want to meet my sisters without visiting Spain? Si? They come here to London?" he quizzed.

"No, no, no, Javier!" snapped Daniel with frustration. "Stop! Listen to me. Do you remember Lady Catherine, Sir Herbert Frankland's daughter?"

"Oooh" Si, Señor! The lady from Hampshire? Who could forget the most beautiful woman in England?"

"Yes, that one," Daniel sighed mournfully.

"I ordered a housekeeper from the agency on Piccadilly. You know the one. It has an excellent reputation for supplying loyal staff. I wanted someone to keep things clean and tidy when I am away. It gets in such a dusty mess when I am on a dig. And when I am back, I thought I could have a few meals cooked when I was busy lecturing and wanted to eat at home. The agency sent a note telling me they had found the perfect person. Her name was Catherine Carter. She was young, literate, and I could easily train her. She sounded ideal."

"Oh no, Daniel. Don't tell me—this Miss Catherine Carter—is Lady Catherine?"

"Yes. The very same!"

Javier's chin dropped.

"So, what did you do?"

"I was so shocked to see her that I got dressed and came here as fast as I could."

"You came all this way just to ask for advice about your love life from this old bachelor?"

"No, I came to mark some exam papers, but I cannot concentrate anymore. I need your advice," begged Daniel displaying unusual drama.

"Women cause problems, Daniel, stay a bachelor. There are plenty of women who think like men if you see what I mean? Why not take a woman who can love you in the afternoon and be gone by dinner?" lectured Javier. "It happens all the time. It keeps things nice and simple."

"You don't understand, Javier. She let me go. I asked her to leave Hampshire with me, and I promised her everything. I am sure she felt the same spark between us. She even came to see me in my bed—and no, nothing happened—before you ask."

"You did not tell me any of this, my friend."

"She said she could not marry me, and she had to marry that pig farmer Sebastian Pimbleby. Remember him?"

"Si, the ugly little bulldog," Javier confirmed.

Daniel nodded.

"At least you did not make love to Catherine, Daniel. At least you cannot remember the pleasure of her body," said Javier, ever the over-romantic emotional Spaniard.

"That is the problem, Javier. We got close to—let's just say I remember the pleasure of being alone with her."

"You do? You did? How alone?" his eyes growing wider.

"Enough for me to fall head over heels for her from a distance for three years. Now, she is working in my house."

"Ah, but that night was such a long time ago, Daniel. You will easily find another woman."

"I do not want another woman. In all those years, Javier, nobody has ever moved me the way she did. She walked into my Mayfair house, looked at me with those large grey eyes, and all the memories come flooding back—and the humiliation of her choosing the bulldog over me."

"Love is never simple, Daniel, but everybody says it is worth it. I must confess, I have yet to be convinced," he added with a cheeky smile.

"Do you know where she is staying?"

"Piecing together some details from the agency, I believe she is staying in the God-forsaken hole that is the Old Nichol of all places."

"Really! The tenements over by Whitechapel?"

"Yes."

"Well, Daniel," said Javier seriously, "there must be a very long story behind this if she has moved in there. I hear some dreadful tales of what goes on in that den of depravity. Even the police are reluctant to wander the alleyways there. Where is Sebastian?"

"I have no idea. Anyway, it is of no consequence. I have decided the answer is to fire her."

"Not so fast, Daniel."

"How so?"

"Perhaps you should take her to bed first—finish off what you started!"

Javier laughed loudly at his mischief.

"This is not funny, Javier," chastised Daniel.

"Si, si, I just made a little joke. If it were me, Daniel, I would just make love to the beautiful Catherine, marry her and have many babies."

An exasperated Daniel shook his head in frustration. *Damned Latino lotharios. They never understand!*

Daniel left Javier's office feeling worse rather than better. He knew that no matter how much he promised to fire Catherine, he was only fooling himself. *I don't care if she was forced to sleep with Pimbleby out of wedlock.*

She was hardly picking up men from the street! Besides, if she had laid with ten other men, I wouldn't have cared. It's her I want. She is my soulmate. Society's rules be damned. Surely, she is spirited enough to see things my way?

Daniel had dreamed about Catherine many a night since the weekend in Hampshire. She was the first person he thought about when he awoke in the morning. Every time he was intimate with another woman, he imagined that it was her. Yet, when she stood in front of him this morning, he did not know what to say or do.

He walked home from the station, unaware of anything happening around him. Feeling anxious and confused, he was desperate to regain control of his life. He turned the key in the apartment lock, wondering what—and who—he would encounter. The place was empty, and that disappointed him. The curtains were drawn, and he lit the lamps to see if anything had changed.

Everything was the same as he had left it that morning. The books stood in untidy heaps. His desk was a mess. *But now—it is a clean mess. She's followed my instructions to the letter. Look, she's even put my post on my desk.*

There was food in the kitchen, some strange things that he had never eaten before. He decided to play it safe and nibbled on some chunky bread with fresh butter. It tasted delicious. Then he put a pot of his favourite Turkish coffee on the stove and waited for the lovely smell to permeate the rooms while he went to his study to open his letters.

The top few envelopes contained receipts for the food that Catherine had bought. There was an envelope with an Egyptian postage stamp which he put to one side. He opened a letter from the Foreign Office granting him permission him to travel to Gibraltar. He planned to meet world-famous Sheikh Ali Mohammed from Morocco, a renowned Arab archaeologist. Another note confirmed his passage was booked, and he would leave in a few days. At the bottom of the pile was a note, a simple piece of paper folded in half with his name on it. *It's from her.* Carefully, he unfurled the letter and read it.

> *Daniel,*
>
> *There has been a terrible mistake.*
>
> *Please accept my resignation.*
>
> *Yours always,*
>
> *Catherine*

Daniel rolled the note into a ball and threw it across the study. *That wretched woman has done it again. Thrown me a tantalising bone, hasn't she? 'Yours always'. Where the hell has that idea come from? She keeps her cards close to her chest, that one.*

He began savouring his coffee. *At least that never lets me down!* Halfway through it, he stood up and started searching for the crumpled note. Eventually, he found it between a pile of books on Japan and ancient manuscripts from Persia. He opened it once more and reread it. *'Yours always'. He* folded it and put it into his pocket. *I suppose I should keep this for a while.*

Daniel could not sleep. Every time he started to doze, Catherine would flit to mind, and he would be wide awake once more. Eventually, he gave up and lay looking at the ceiling and wondering what to do. Javier's words came back to him, and he smiled. *'Love is never simple, but everybody says that it is worth it.' Bloody romantic Europeans.*

Daniel was up, washed and dressed by six o'clock, but it was too early to do anything about his aching heart. He sat down at his desk and tried to read the letter from Gibraltar, but he lost his concentration halfway through it and gave up. He drank one cup of coffee after the next, and at seven-thirty, he decided to make his way across the West End to the staffing agency in Piccadilly.

He sat in front of a formidable middle-aged woman, who insisted on acknowledging him as 'Professor.'

"Mrs Jesson, you sent me a housekeeper named Catherine Carter," Daniel stated.

"Yes, professor. She started work for you at the beginning of last week, I believe. Is there a problem?" asked the woman.

"Yes. She resigned," Daniel said candidly.

"Oh!" She exclaimed, looking him up and down, trying to decide if his behaviour was the root of the problem. "Did she do something wrong, professor?"

Her eyes were boring into Daniel, and it was clear she was inferring that he was at fault, not her recruitment process or the calibre of her applicants.

"No, not at all. Her work has been exemplary. I got home yesterday evening from the university, and my apartment was cleaned from top to bottom. I thought she had finished for the day and gone home. I sat down to attend to some business and found a note on my desk, stating her resignation. I need to find her."

"I cannot give out staff addresses on a whim. It is not our policy, professor. I am sure you understand."

Daniel put his head in his hands in frustration. *Everyone seems to delight in raising my blood pressure of late. Have I been struck by an ancient temple curse or something?*

"I still want her to work for me," he said with a sigh.

"I appreciate you are happy with the standard of her work, Professor Leicester. However, I cannot guarantee that she will want to continue working for you. As you know, she is well-educated for someone from Whitechapel, and she will work for a very modest wage. She can have her pick of any household in the area. Why would she come back to you if she has made her wishes clear—and in writing."

Daniel stood up, abruptly and plunged his hand into his pocket, fished out the note and unfolded it.

"Here! Read it! You can see she is labouring under a misapprehension. There has been no mistake. She must have needed the money else why apply for the job? And you will lose your fee from me for finding her."

Mrs Jesson read the note, keeping her eyes down as she pondered Catherine's decision. *Yours always? What a strange way to end a resignation. He doesn't seem the sort to put the frighteners on a girl the first day he meets her. What shall I do?*

A queue was forming in the reception area. The impatient faces staring through the glass window were urging her to deal with the current matter so she could resolve theirs.

"Very well. Just this once, I shall give you Miss Carter's address. However, should she report any trouble from you, I will need to bring that to the attention of the authorities. We as a reputable agency we are very particular about the wellbeing of our workers."

"Thank you, Mrs Jesson. I shall respect yours and Miss Carter's wishes. You have my solemn word."

She wrote down Catherine's address and gave it to him.

"Oh, and good luck, professor," she said with a worrying tone. "You will be searching through hell itself to find her."

9

THE SLUM VISIT

"Janey! Janey! Open up," cried Catherine thumping on her neighbour's door early the following morning after enduring a sleepless night.

"What is it petal? You making all this noise n'all? It's a good job that I haven't got a gentleman caller."

"Something terrible has happened," wailed Catherine pushing the door wide open and marching into the room.

"What's happened? Why are ye in such a shambles?"

"I don't have a job, Janey, and I have to start all over again. I am so very tired of being forced to start again!" lamented Catherine.

"Blimey, lass! What did yer do to get fired so soon?" laughed Janey, trying to lighten the mood. "I thought ye would make a bad housemaid. Did you knock a precious vase off a shelf this morning when you were dusting?"

"Bless your heart for having so much faith in me and my dusting skills, Janey," huffed Catherine. "As a matter of fact, I didn't make any blunders. I resigned."

"Resigned? But I thought you was doin' so well like! You managed a whole week without getting the bullet," she chuckled. "What has gotten into yer head? Can I make ye a cuppa, lass? That'll cheer you up."

"Oh, yes, please. That will be lovely."

"So why did ye leave then? Not allowed to be on the gin at work?"

"Very funny. No, I got to the apartment this morning, and I had the fright of my life," Catherine sighed. "Do you remember I told you about Professor Leicester, Daniel, who I came so close to having an affair with that weekend when he visited our family home?"

Janey nodded. *How could I forget? You're always mentioning him being a country mile better than Sebastian.*

"Well, the apartment is his—Daniel's—London residence! The woman at the agency did not give me a name, only told me to report to 'the professor.' Mr Farley only talked about 'the professor.' Well, it was quite a shock to find out it was him. I could not stay, all those memories of spurning him. I am so embarrassed. I can't even look at him. It was awful."

"Aww, love. Did he recognise yer?"

"Yes, he did. Of course, he did. But today, he hardly spoke to me. It was as if he wanted to be cold and distant to deliberately hurt me. To make me understand he thought nothing of me, I suppose? Well, it seemed that way to me. He rushed off to the university and told me to change nothing and just clean. Couldn't get away from me fast enough."

"Humph. Toffs, eh? Always thinking of themselves."

"No, Janey, he's not like that at all." Catherine found herself defending him, and it put her on edge. "I could have married him. He asked me, but I was too afraid after what Sebastian did to me. I told Daniel what happened at the garden party, and he didn't seem to care. I didn't want his name tarnished. Sebastian was horribly vindictive back then. Who knows how he would have retaliated?"

"Aww, Catherine. Ye know us common folk are different. If it were the man I loved, I would have walked right up to him and given him what for fer taking so fekking long to find me, nor fekking run away!" Janey giggled.

"Stop cursing. It's not helping!"

"Yes, ma'am," chortled Janey. Doubled up with laughter, she curtsied so low her nose almost collided with her knees.

"If yer still in love with him, go back."

"Who said anything about love, Janey?" said Catherine defensively.

"Well lass, in the years ye been me, neighbour, ye talk about that professor daily."

"I don't."

"Yes, yer do! Ain't it time yer just gave in and owned up to it?"

Catherine stared into her teacup.

"He can be quite forthright. In a sense, it is charming. I do worry what might happen if he lost his temper? What if he turns into another

Sebastian—a man who prefers to speak with his fists."

Catherine went quiet. Janey was desperate to say more but bit her tongue.

"I can't forget that night together, Janey. Lying in his arms, I did not want to let him go. I could think of nothing else but leaving with him rather than having to dread my future with that monster Sebastian. I felt safe with Daniel. But you know what Sebastian said. He would ruin my family—and he meant it."

"Lass, look at yersel'! Yer lives in this hellhole to escape another hellhole. What's happened to yer backbone? Facing Daniel Leicester can be no worse than leaving that scoundrel ye' married or living in Whitechapel."

Catherine put her cup down.

"I can't make you another brew, petal. The priest's due soon. Monday's his day. He always needs to unwind after hearing all those saucy confessions from the Irish dockers over the weekend," she sniggered.

With that, Catherine made a swift departure. She slumped down on her rickety bed, with the weight of the world bearing down on her shoulders. She changed out of her uniform and resolved to take it back to Mrs Jesson. *It's unlikely she'll give me a second chance either.*

Flouncing off so soon like that must have created a terrible impression.

Outside, the day had turned dark, broody. The rain fell like stair rods. Daniel sidestepped the gritty black water as it swept down the slight slope towards St. Paul's. *Not far now. Keep going.* It looked as if dusk was settling over Whitechapel, but it was only eleven o'clock in the morning.

Daniel was soaked. He had foolishly left his brolly behind. Muttering, he swore under his breath. Many grey, ragged-looking people were pushing their way up and down the lanes in a hurry to get to their destinations. Others remained under the arches, shop doorways and any other places they could shelter. Quite a few looked like they lived on the streets. No matter what the weather threw at those people, Daniel sensed there would never be any respite. *What if Catherine ends up homeless if Mrs Jesson doesn't find her another appointment? It will all be my fault.*

Daniel could not bear to see the real England. The England of the working class—the jobless, the sick, the poor and the destitute. The England of no hope and no glory where men worked in the most dreadful conditions to fuel the industrial revolution and the empire that made men like his father and Sir Rufus rich.

Except for a good pair of shoes, Daniel was wearing the same clothes as the workers. He found them more practical. On a dig site, there would be no point prancing around in the latest men's expensive and vulgar fashions. *The tight trousers, the coats and tails and those bloody awful top hats. Who dreamt them up? So impractical for a working man.*

Daniel pulled his cap low over his eyes and his coat collar up towards his ears to shield himself from the rain. He felt the piece of paper with the address in his pocket, shielding it in the palm of his hand to keep it dry. *She had better be at this address after all this trouble!*

He saw two young lads lurking at the entrance to a factory. He was fairly confident they weren't the sort to garrotte him down an alleyway and rob him blind. *Please let this be a short visit. How can Catherine live in such a place?*

"You lads live around here?" he asked in a gruff voice.

"Yes, squire," answered one.

"Wadda yer want wiv us, mister?" asked his friend.

"I'm looking for an address."

Daniel pulled out the piece of paper and read it to them.

They looked at each other and nodded.

"Yeah, we know where it is."

"I will give you each a shilling when we reach it."

"Nah, mister, that won't do it. All the risk's on us. One shilling now. One when we get there."

Daniel nodded, and the boys developed broad grins.

"And don't think of pick-pocketing me. I know you little rotters are up to no good. I know a finger-smith when I see one," he said in his best intimidating voice.

The boys realised that this fellow somehow knew his way around the streets, even if he looked out of place. They immediately adopted a more respectful manner with him.

"Sir, come wiv us, Sir. We'll take ye. We won't be no bother. Promise ye that."

"Good. That's settled then. Shall we make a move, lads? I would like to get there before Christmas!"

The boys didn't move a muscle until a shilling was dropped into their grubby, cupped hands.

The trio didn't walk far, but even with directions, Daniel would have been lost in the maze of alleys and streets. There were no street names to be seen. They suddenly stopped by a small entrance, which was lacked a solid door. Instead, a bit of coal sack made into a makeshift curtain flapped in the wind.

"In here. Along the ginnel to the courtyard, then up the stairs, mister," they chorused.

He gave the boys their second shilling each. They didn't move again.

"Thank you, lads. I can find my way back. Now, scoot""

"Sure, mister?"

"Very."

Everything in the street became a glistening jet black as soot washed down the sides of the former red brick buildings. He could not imagine what had possessed Catherine to come and live in this godforsaken place.

On his way through the slum, he heard the wailing of infants and the screaming of mothers. Occasionally, he got a glimpse inside a house when their simple curtain doors fluttered to one side. The facilities looked meagre. Often five or six men were sitting about in the small rooms, talking and drinking. Hungry-looking children stood in the doorways trying to stay warm, and barefoot paupers walked from door to door asking for food.

Daniel continued through the alley between two tenements and reached a muddy courtyard the lads had described. He smelled the privies before he saw them.

There were four for the whole block where Catherine lived. The midden was overflowing in the rain, and the stench was so vile he wanted to vomit. During the time he spent in Cairo, he never experienced anything as dehumanising as this.

He climbed two flights of stairs and checked the number on the note. It was pointless—there were no signs on the doors. Daniel decided to knock on every door. Eventually, at what he guessed was number six, he got an answer. A woman in her late twenties opened the door. He noticed she was attractive in a rough, bawdy way.

"So, you've got here, at last, have you? Took yer bloody time too didnya, now?"

Her overly presumptuous greeting threw Daniel for a moment. He blurted out his mission.

"Excuse me. I am looking for—"

"—Yes, ye are lookin' for Catherine aren't yer, mate?" the woman interrupted.

"But?"

Daniel wasn't quite sure why the woman seemed to know him at first then it dawned on him. *Catherine must have spoken about me.* He took that to be a good sign.

Janey looked him up and down like a docker would eye up a pretty woman. *Catherine was right. He is most dashing. Tall. Very good looking—in a dark, brooding way.* He had a commanding presence even though she had not heard him speak more than a few words. A man in his mid-thirties, he was no longer a boy. She could see why Catherine was in love with the fellow—compared with Janey's punters, she thought Daniel Leicester was stunning.

"She's next door, flower. Ye better take her wiv yer, fella. This is no place for a lady."

"Thank you," Daniel whispered with an alluring smile.

Janey pointed to the entrance opposite, then went about her business, closing her door with its distinctive creak. He gave Catherine's door a soft knock.

"Come in, Janey."

Daniel opened the door quietly and stepped into the room. An iron cot bed stood in the corner, the bedding threadbare. A stove was burning, which was more decorative than practical as it struggled to keep the place warm. The broken window leaked badly. Water was pooling on the warped sill, then trickling down the wall. The rags stuffed into the jagged hole where the pane should be seemed to wick in more moisture than keep it out. Catherine's clothes hung across the room on a piece of rope. He saw her standing next to a deep wooden tub up to her elbows in suds hard at work. She stopped briefly to see what Janey wanted then froze. *What is he doing here?*

"Daniel?" she quizzed coldly.

"I have come to fetch you."

"Why? I don't need your charity."

Daniel stood with his hands in his pockets and watched her.

"I don't feel sorry for you, Catherine. I am merely suggesting you will be more comfortable at my apartment."

"I am comfortable here."

Annoyed, he splashed his fingers in the water that was collecting on the window sill to indicate her living conditions were anything but comfortable. *She is the most impossible woman I have ever met.*

He was cold and hungry. After walking through hell itself to find her, he had better things to do than tolerate her stubborn mood. *Why is she still denying the attraction? It's been there since Lymington. She felt it. I felt it. Why did blasted Sebastian have to ruin everything?*

"I suppose you want me back in your bed if you want me at your apartment?"

He fought hard to hide his true feelings, dreading scaring her away again if he were intense.

"Catherine, I don't want you in my bed. I don't even know if I want you in my life."

His voice was deep and even, his tone devoid of emotion.

"Quite simply, I see it as my duty to your father to help you find a better place to live. This has got nothing to do with romance. This is reality." He paused. "—I presume Sir Herbert has no idea you are here? He would be mortified."

Facing the truth sobered Catherine, and she stopped arguing briefly. Daniel was relieved. Janey came into the room and stood behind the professor.

"Pack your stuff, lass. Go with him. He's right. If it was me, I'd bite his hand off for an offer like that," advised Janey.

"But—I can't leave you, Jane."

"Aw come now. Of course, ye can, I'm a big girl who can look after herself. Besides I've got a thriving business to run," she said with a mischievous grin.

A jittery Catherine began to pack her few clothes into a suitcase. Janey stepped in to help. Daniel did not say a word to her, but when she was finished, he picked up the suitcase and walked toward the door. Catherine hoped it was a secret sign of affection and not a purely gentlemanly gesture.

"Yer will look after her well, Daniel?" enquired Janey.

"Yes," he answered firmly, giving no real clue to his intentions, romantic or otherwise. "Thank you for your help."

Daniel hired a cab, and he and Catherine rode across the city in silence. He was relieved to see the back of Whitechapel. The squalor and deprivation depressed him. There were four miles between Whitechapel, a grotesque slum that housed the poorest of the poor, and the glory and splendour of Buckingham Palace, the home of one of the wealthiest women in the world. Victoria had an empire that stretched almost around the world, but many of her subjects lived in abject poverty right under her nose.

Daniel was often tempted to give away some of the vast family fortune to some philanthropic endeavour or other. For a long time, he had longed to escape the world of the rich. Now, this journey into the East End felt like the catalyst. As the bleak streets drifted by the carriage window, Daniel was lost in thought, mulling over his options. *Perhaps I shall waive my inheritance and sign it over to my middle brother. I have more than sufficient means to take care of myself, and I will build an honest life, free of the fussy trappings that accompany aristocratic life.*

Sir and Lady Leicester would be furious with him, of course, but he had a reputation as a wild eccentric, and he often liked to milk it. He was tired of being constrained and itched to be free of the family's —and society's—bothersome rules.

By the time they reached Daniel's apartment, he looked like a thundercloud. Catherine, misunderstanding up on his bristly mood, was regretting leaving Janey behind.

Mr Farley greeted the new arrival cheerfully. She gave him a weak smile in return.

> "You will sleep in my bed, Miss Carter. I will make space for myself in the sitting room," ordered Daniel.

Deciding he was angry, she made no attempt to argue with him. Instead, she observed him. There was something attractive about a man who took control of his environment without violence or venom.

For once, she had carte blanche to do whatever she pleased. Better still, she knew that the woman who won Daniel's heart would be protected and cherished. *Could that person ever be me? Our special night in Lymington seems like a lifetime away. Is this arrangement convenience, or commitment?*

Catherine unpacked her meagre belongings. Daniel stuck his head around the door.

> "There is a laundress that collects my clothes. Include yours in the bundle. I suggest you go out and get yourself some new attire. I will send the bill to your father."

She saw that last comment for the white lie that it was. It was clear Daniel would be footing the bill. Guilt and hope intermingled in her mind.

"I don't expect to live here for free. I have to earn my keep while I am staying."

"You will. I have plenty for you to do. I will give you a daily list of chores. I did employ a domestic to help me before, remember?"

Catherine nodded, then tried to spend the rest of the day as far from Daniel as possible, keeping herself busy with chores well away from the study.

After an awkward evening meal, they both retired to their beds in silence.

The next morning, the storm that had drenched the city had blown over, to be replaced by a delightful sunny day. The bright yellowy light shone on the buildings, and outside at least, the warmth clearly uplifted everybody's moods. Inside Daniel's apartment, it was dark and gloomy. The dark heavy furniture, an abundance of leather chairs and several old carpets stole the brightness of the beautiful weather outside.

Daniel, however, was not there. He had left early. Catherine overheard him tell Farley he had some errands to attend to at the university. She kept herself busy crossing off items on Daniel's lengthy to-do list that Farley had handed to her at nine o'clock sharp.

"Let us go and sit in the sunshine, Javier," said Daniel.

They chose a stone bench in one of the university's courtyards and sat silently for a few minutes, absorbing the warmth. Javier suspected Daniel had something on his mind.

"I am leaving for Gibraltar in the next few days. The department is sending me to look at a newly discovered set of chambers connected to St. Michael's cave. It is a significant site, and they want me to manage the excavation process. It is suspected there are more prehistoric tools to be discovered that will need careful logging. Then the government plans to use the space to store munitions."

"I am envious, my friend. All those señoritas in the Mediterranean sunshine," said Javier with a smile.

"Well, there is still a complication for me when it comes to señoritas."

"There is?" said Javier, playing dumb.

"I rescued Catherine from the jaws of Whitechapel yesterday. She is staying at my apartment."

"You are going to be the talk of the town, Señor Daniel," he chuckled.

"I don't damned well care, Javier. They can talk all they like."

"Will it affect her reputation?"

"I think she has already destroyed her reputation; leaving her husband and disappearing like she has for three years, don't you?"

Javier nodded.

"You know that I don't care about that. Our society fools itself that women and men are chaste until marriage. It is all a Victorian myth."

"You have a grieving Queen Victoria, we have the Roman Catholic Church to clip our wings of passion," smiled Javier.

Daniel nodded.

"Do you still love her, Daniel?"

"Of course, I still love her. You know that!" he protested. "Even if she is the most challenging woman I have ever met."

Javier smirked at his romantic dilemma.

"Look, Javier, there are plenty of women in the world with whom I can amuse myself. I am not sure I want to complicate my life with just one. Besides, she is still married. And she upped sticks and ran away from her family. If that's isn't complication, I don't know what is. I have sent a telegram to her father this morning, telling him that she is safe, by the way. He was thrilled to hear it. His response was telling. Sir Herbert told me that Pimbleby Pig farmer fellow is looking for her and wants her back. If somebody recognises her in London and word gets out, Sebastian will fetch her—and who knows what will happen then. He is not going to breathe a word about her reappearance until her safety can be guaranteed."

"When I said that women can turn your life upside down—"

Daniel interrupted, not in the mood for another of his friend's lessons of the heart.

"—I can't leave her alone in London, Javier. Do you think I should risk taking her with me to Gibraltar?"

"My friend, I believe you have already made your decision, and you just need confirmation from me. Si, Daniel. Take her with you. It is what you want."

"You know me too well, old friend. Thank you."

Daniel returned home to find his apartment smelled like a delicious bakery. Fresh scones were on a plate in the kitchen. He noted Catherine had made his bed on the couch in front of the fire.

"Since when could you bake?" he asked Catherine.

"I watched the street vendors. I have learnt a lot from them."

"I am sure that you have."

"That and Mrs Farley gave me a copy of Mrs Beeton's Book of Household Management," she added with a smile that went unnoticed.

Daniel had turned away, spooning some coffee into his Turkish pot. He poured the rich brown liquid into two small cups while Catherine set up the table for afternoon tea.

"You are coming with me to Gibraltar. We will be travelling by steamer in a few days."

"I beg your pardon?"

"I have been requested to work on a large-scale dig. I will need help over there while I am away."

"You told the agency you needed help here when you were away. I am perfectly happy to stay in London," she snapped, the surprise offer to accompany him overseas confusing her. "I do not need a babysitter, Daniel."

Here we go again. Her damn pride and independence will be the death of me.

"There is plenty to do in this place. I can keep myself busy."

"It's an instruction, not a request, Catherine. If you want to be useful, make sure that your bags are packed. I am not giving you a choice."

"You cannot tell me what to do Daniel. I did not ask for you to fetch me."

"Do you have money to fend for yourself?"

"No." she snapped. "You know that!"

"If you want to leave, you can work yourself out of the hole you are in. I won't charge you rent here. Until you have saved up enough money, you'll have to do as I say."

"I was happy in Whitechapel," she yelled at him, feeling trapped again.

"You were about to be evicted, and the next step would have been stepping into Janey's profession to survive, or live under a bridge," Daniel chided.

"How do you know about, Janey's profession?" asked Catherine in irritation.

"Catherine, I have been around the world, I know a kind-hearted fallen woman when I see one."

"That 'fallen woman' is my friend," said Catherine, annoyed that he was so judgemental.

"I know she is, and you can be her friend for the rest of your life. She is poor, and she does what she must to survive. I am sorry for belittling her," he said with sincerity.

Catherine nodded in acceptance of the apology.

"I really would value your help with the administrative work in Gibraltar. You are an archaeologist's daughter, after all. You are more useful to me over there than staying here. As you know, if I take a student with me, they will see it as more of an excuse to have a jolly overseas than the important work it is. Have your bags packed. I am leaving the day after tomorrow—and you are coming with me. Agreed?"

He didn't wait for an answer. Finishing his coffee, he went into the study, leaving Catherine to pinch herself as she pondered the dramatic change of events. *Is there more to his offer than meets the eye? How I would love to tell Janey. I can imagine what she would say about it.* She chuckled as she rinsed the coffee cups. *Life is never dull with Daniel Leicester about, that's for sure.*

10

SEBASTIAN RECEIVES HIS ORDERS

Sebastian Pimbleby strode into his mother's home with the arrogance of an angry peacock. He shoved his coat and hat at the butler and waved him off dismissively. The old servant wasn't surprised, the young upstart had always had bad manners since he was a petulant toddler.

Pimbleby then marched down the hall and stormed into the morning room. His mother had summoned him, which for him was never a good sign. Dreading the encounter, he wanted to get away from her as fast as possible. He found his mother difficult. She delighted in showering him with pointed questions that he did not or could not answer.

"Good morning, mother," he greeted in an overconfident voice to mask his anxiety.

"And to you, Sebastian," said Lady Pimbleby in clipped aristocratic tones.

"Where is father?"

"He is in London, staying at his club," she answered haughtily. "As a matter of fact, I received a telegram from him yesterday afternoon."

"You did?" enquired Sebastian.

"Yes. All our family has been invited to an elite event at Buckingham Palace. They are paying attention to the southern counties at last, not just the industrial north."

"Oh, jolly good show. The palace. I am impressed," said Sebastian, his ego suitably flattered.

"And then we have been invited to Royal Ascot. We will be accommodated in the Royal Box. This is a significant social milestone for the Pimblebys."

"How fabulous mother. It is a step up from this dogged remote country life. A chance to meet with so many powerful families will be a blessing."

There was a long silence as Lady Pimbleby poured out a second cup of breakfast tea.

"But we do have a problem, Sebastian."

"We do?"

Once more, her son's conduct made Lady Pimbleby tut in frustration.

"Yes. A problem of your making. You need to find your wife. There is no possibility of you attending without her."

"Mother, how many times have I told you this? I have had investigators search the country from end to end. I cannot find Catherine. I am convinced that she has left England. I was thinking of contacting the Pinkerton Agency. She may have settled in New York."

"That is a ridiculous conclusion," she admonished. "When last did you speak to the Franklands?"

"I have not spoken to them for a year, mother. Lady Anna will not even acknowledge my letters or formal invitations to meet. For some reason, they want nothing to do with me."

"Neither would I if I were them."

Sebastian glared at his mother.

"Don't look at me like that, Sebastian. You know full and well that you were cruel to Catherine and you drove her into exile."

"Oh, mother, what a lie that is. I have no idea what has given you that idea. You cannot trust the servants' gossip."

"Really Sebastian? Did you know she sought my help? If I had known then that her leaving would have brought such shame on the family, I would have stepped in and taken control of you well before then."

"Mother, she is my wife and 'managing her' was within my remit, not yours. As a fiercely headstrong woman, she needed to learn some manners," Sebastian said arrogantly.

"Perhaps so, Sebastian, but you chose a poor way to manage your wild child wife. You made her hate you."

"I did not!" argued Sebastian loudly, but not daring to shout.

"Of course, you did," countered Lady Pimbleby.

"It is all gossip, cheap servant's gossip, mother."

"And is it gossip that there was a dead white stallion in your barn on the night that she left? Does a good husband shoot his wife's beloved horse in the head in cold blood?"

Sebastian looked down at his feet.

"You shot that horse to spite her, didn't you? Even I had an appreciation for that magnificent animal, and you know my thoughts on all matters equestrian."

After suffering such a lengthy dressing down from his mother, Sebastian dare not say a word. Unfortunately for him, Lady Pimbleby was just getting started.

"You are a disgrace, Sebastian! I am going to give you a task and woe betide you if you fail. Find your wife. Then, make her the happiest woman in England. Treat her like a princess. I will never forgive you for bringing us under such scrutiny. I loathe having to cover up for your mistake. If we miss out on this opportunity to visit the palace, you too will find yourself 'in exile'."

"Can't we just say she's ill? Bedridden with a difficult pregnancy?" Sebastian stammered.

"Catherine is the daughter of Sir Herbert Frankland. What will it look like if we are at the same gathering, and her husband and father have differing opinions about her situation? You will find her, and you will bring her to the palace event. Is that understood?"

"Yes, mother."

For all his bravado, Sebastian left the room with his tail between his legs.

After she had fled their home, Sebastian hired a private investigator to search for her in London, not the length and breadth of the country like he told his mother. He invested in the agent's services for several months, but the man could produce nothing. Sebastian felt little remorse over the disappearance of Catherine because he was still married to her on paper—which meant that he still had the full benefit of the union. Her presence or absence made little difference to him.

Why was mother so het up about it? Wasn't it 'old news?'

Socially, Sebastian was considered the wronged party. He received a lot of sympathy from his friends throughout the elite over the months and years. After all, a decent woman did not run away from her husband. There were other far more agreeable ways that she could have dealt with unhappiness: long trips to the colonies, travel through Europe with an entourage, a house in Scotland where she could discreetly entertain a lover or two. Catherine was not the first aristocratic wife to take flight.

Nevertheless, in English society, when the season opened, you were expected to be with your wife unless she was dead. Tired of making coordinated excuses, with the biggest social event of the century landing in the lap of Sir and Lady Pimbleby, having a missing daughter-in-law was not an option. They decided they would no longer tolerate Sebastian's handling of the situation.

Daniel and Catherine began their journey to Gibraltar by travelling to Hampshire at night. Catherine listened to the soft puffing of the steam engine and the rhythmic clickety-clack of its wheels. Except for those two comforts, she was terrified of going to Southampton. She had overcome the temptation to visit her parents, consoling herself with the fact that they knew Daniel was looking after her and that she was safer than she had been for quite some time.

Catherine did not tell Daniel her fears about Sebastian hunting her down, but subtle clues in her demeanour made it obvious to him. He was clearly concerned too. He had engineered their travel plans to be as discreet as possible. He did not fear meeting Sebastian Pimbleby, but Catherine did—and his chief objective was to protect her. He looked at her beautiful yet vigilant face, staring out into the blackness outside. He thought back to that one innocent night together, when she had fallen asleep with her head on his chest. A tenderness overwhelmed him. He wanted to wrap his arms around her and tell her that he would protect her forever but managed to retain his composure.

While Daniel watched Catherine, he summed up his life, weighing up the wisdom of a relationship with her. He was an upper-class academic about to forsake his considerable inheritance to wrestle his future from his father. At some point, Catherine would need to face the real world. If she divorced her husband or married Daniel, she would be a social outcast. Perhaps, if she chose a life in a Hampshire backwater, in time, she would become comfortable and more importantly—accepted. That wasn't guaranteed by any means.

Daniel could not identify a single event that caused him to detest the class structure. His archaeological studies had taught him there were other, fairer, ways to structure a society. As a young child, he squirmed at the way his mother and father spoke to their servants. For them, it might have been a working arrangement, but for him, these were the people who had loved him and raised him in the shadows of his parents' grand lifestyle. That his parents thought it acceptable to rule with an iron rod, to hurt and humiliate them daily, barely recognise them as humans, well it rankled him.

He would secretly meet up with the local boys down at the river or in the fields, but woe betide him if he attempted to bring a village child to the family home. The Leicesters called themselves 'Christians', yet for Daniel, they failed to uphold the compassionate values of the Lord. Tired of attempting and failing to have a meaningful social or religious debate with his parents, he was done with his home life. In fact, with the spirited Catherine beside him who seemed equally tired of a life crammed with endless trivial rules, he felt quite ready to relinquish the treasured benefits of being the first-born son to his other siblings.

Snapping out of his thoughts, once more, he redirected his focus to the more pressing matter of caring for Catherine now. He watched her asleep in her seat. For once, she was quiet. Her head had fallen to one side, and a piece of hair fell over her face. He reached out and tucked it behind her ear. She sighed in her sleep. He remembered the first time he tried to kiss her as she rode that magnificent Arabian. I should have tried harder. I should have fought for her. I should have saved her from Pimbleby.

Alone with his thoughts, he felt full of regret.

Daniel sat slumped over with his elbows on his knees and his head in his hands. His tall physique was feeling uncomfortable in the cramped carriage. He was looking forward to the voyage to Gibraltar, at least they could stroll about on deck if the weather was fine. He missed the warm sun and open skies and hoped that Catherine would enjoy the sense of freedom and adventure too.

In the early morning, they found the Port of Southampton was buzzing with activity. Amidst the considerable shouting, sailors, porters and chandlers lined the wharfs loading cargo onto the ships. Catherine stood at Daniel's side, soaking up the experience. She felt the thrill of the adventure, and she could not wait to board the ship. Out of the corner of his eye, Daniel picked up on her sense of wanderlust, and his heart skipped a beat. He handed her the tickets. Catherine inspected them with interest.

"A merchant ship?" she asked.

"Yes. It's cheaper, and we don't have to
tolerate society bores," he chuckled. "You
won't be bored," he promised, "some
fascinating people travel cattle class."

She handed the tickets back, and Daniel carefully slotted them back in his trouser pocket.

The morning sunlight bathed them as they stood on the dockside, waiting for the call to board. The brisk walk from the station helped warm them too. Daniel had taken off his jacket and rolled his sleeves up. His shirttails were hanging out of his trousers. With his fedora sat at an angle, Catherine thought he looked perfect.

"Over here, Professor."

Daniel had been called to sign the manifest, confirming that all his research equipment was on board. Catherine looked at all the crates and wondered what might be in them. Daniel towered above the other men on the pier and smiled good-naturedly when they addressed him. She noted this seemed like home to him. He was a breath of fresh air compared with the stuffiness of her upbringing, and the tight-laced Pimblebys trying far too hard to impress. It was the moment when she accepted that she was in love with the free spirit called Professor Daniel Leicester, and somehow, she would win him over. *One day, I will be more than his housekeeper or dig assistant.*

With his paperwork complete, Daniel returned to keep a watchful eye over his travelling companion.

A man in a fine suit stood a way behind them on the dock. He was looked old and haggard. His face was bright pink face, bordered by a fuzzy white beard. A big fat stomach made the gold buttons strain on his dark overcoat.

"You, boy!" the old man shouted at the steward. "Yes, you. Come over here."

"Sir?" the steward enquired politely.

He pointed at Catherine and Daniel with his walking stick.

"Who are those two over there?"

"I don't know, sir."

"Don't just stand there! Find out. Give me the manifest for that merchant vessel," ordered the grizzly old man.

"I am not allowed to show anybody, sir. I'm sorry. Company policy you see."

"I bet you could show me anything for a pound, boy!" said the old man with a wink, as he jingled some coins in his pocket.

"Quickly then," whispered the steward as he looked around furtively.

The old man studied the manifest. His finger traced its way down to two exciting names. *Well, well, well! If it isn't Daniel Leicester and Catherine Frankland.*

The man handed the steward two pounds.

"It should be one pound, sir," said the steward, impressing the older gentleman with his honesty—after just dishonestly sharing the restricted document. The irony was not lost on either of them.

"Well, you have been so helpful, young man, I think your efforts deserve two."

Dennis Ogilvy could not wait to share his discovery with Pimbleby.

"Sebastian, do you remember the money that I have owed you for such a long time?"

"Yes, of course. You are lucky I haven't broken your legs for it yet."

"I have information that will make your day," revealed Ogilvy, raising his eyebrows conspiratorially.

"Oh, yes? Won on the horses for a change, have you?"

Dennis' good fortune made Pimbleby curious. Ogilvy chuckled, then became more serious.

"If you promise to write off my debt, I will exchange the information."

"I will decide on that, Ogilvy. Get on with it man. What is this blasted news of yours?"

"I was at the port yesterday, and I saw two passengers on the manifest for a merchant ship. I thought you may be interested."

"Who? Spit it out, man," grizzled an impatient Sebastian.

"Daniel Leicester and Catherine Frankland."

"Catherine? You're sure? And she's with him?"

"Yes."

"Where is this ship of theirs heading?"

"Gibraltar," said Ogilvy, feeling important as he relayed his discovery.

"I paid a steward to give me some more information about their passage. He said that they are returning on the same vessel. They'll be back in port in four weeks."

Sebastian Pimbleby smiled from ear to ear. It was the best news he could have received.

"And the debt, sir?" asked Ogilvy without the faintest hint of subtlety.

"Oh, yes, of course. Rest assured we are all square, Mr Ogilvy. And, if this chap of yours has any more information about their whereabouts, I will be happy to pay."

Sebastian was so excited about the development that he went straight to his mother's house.

"What's the meaning of this impromptu visit? Do you have news?"

"Yes, mother," he smiled broadly, "Catherine is on her way to Gibraltar with Daniel Leicester."

"Isn't he that famous archaeologist? A good friend of her father's?"

"Yes, mother."

"I remember you saying that he was at one of those boring lecture parties the Franklands had before you married Catherine."

"Yes, He was. Tall chap. Dark hair."

"Did you get on with the man?" asked Lady Pimbleby.

Sebastian felt uncomfortable.

"I don't know, mother. He ignored me most of the night," he said sheepishly.

"And Catherine, how did he respond to her?"

"He had a brief conversation with her, but otherwise, he showed no interest in her."

"Well," said Lady Pimbleby, "I hope no one else saw her running off with another man. We don't need a bigger mess than we already have."

Sebastian poured himself a stiff drink and stood in front of his mother. His mind went back to the weekend Daniel Leicester had stayed at the Franklands. *Did Daniel seduce Catherine? He had ample opportunity.* Pimbleby felt humiliated. He didn't like Daniel when they first met, and now he seemed to have commandeered his wife. *I wonder how long they have been together? Surely not for three years? He would have to hide her away to keep her secret. Then again, it might explain why she had been so difficult to locate.*

11

THE LONG SAILING

From the moment he stepped off the pier and onto the ship, Daniel was in his element, free of his privileged noose that would choke his freedom if he allowed it. He divided his time onboard between studying and talking to the crew. His days were either spent at a small desk in his cabin or a comfortable chair on the deck. At night he would have dinner with the sailors. Afterwards, they would crack a bottle and play cards or dominoes. Daniel loved to relax with the working men. He delighted in listening to thrilling stories of the distant lands they had sailed to.

The way Catherine spent her time surprised Daniel. She was often on deck, curious to learn more about life at sea from the crew and how the ship worked. She had made friends with the officers and dined in their quarters, and whereas Daniel dined in the general mess. On more than one occasion, he had seen her escorted by Captain Grey. It irked Daniel that it was not his arm that was gallantly steering her around the deck, or offering a steadying hand as she tackled the narrow wooden stairs in a swell. He felt Grey had also fallen under her spell. Daniel's annoyance grew when the captain watched her throw back her head in delightful laughter. It seems *every man on this ship is in love with her. By the time we reach Gibraltar, I am sure her heart will be lost to one of them.*

A few more days into the sailing, the midday sunshine baked the decks. Daniel found Catherine sitting enjoying the weather. She wore a simple floral skirt, a short-sleeved shirt and a big-brimmed straw hat covered her head, her long curly fair hair wafting gently in the breeze. She was relaxed, leaning back in her chair. He could see the contours of her body that filled him with an aching desire—a feeling that could not be bettered despite his many casual dalliances.

Daniel was feeling grumpy. His head was pounding—a result of a boozy party he attended the night before. What's more, his jealousy flared up whenever another sailor acknowledged her as they went about their business. She was like a lighthouse to them, capturing their undivided attention when they passed close by.

"Hello, Daniel," greeted Catherine, radiant and lovely, her grey eyes sparkling like the glittering calm water.

"Catherine," he said coolly, his eyes meeting hers briefly then flitting away towards the horizon.

"What have you been doing? I haven't seen you for ages."

"Working."

"All the time?"

"Yes."

"Every single minute?"

He nodded.

"That's strange. I believe there was quite a party in the general mess last night?" she asked mischievously.

"Yes, there was," he said as he slumped down in the chair next to her.

"Thankfully, I could not hear anything through these thick metal walls. Just the hum of the engine. I slept like a baby."

"Humph," he grunted, noticing his headache worsening as he squinted in the sun.

"Perhaps, you need an early night tonight, to recover from all that—err—work?" said Catherine with a wink.

"Don't advise me on how to live my life, Catherine. And watch yourself with the crew. I've seen you fraternising with them regularly, flirting even. And you let Captain Grey fawn over you in public like a lovesick puppy. There isn't a man's head you haven't turned since we left Southampton. I don't want you embarrassing yourself—or me."

Catherine sat upright in her chair, and her eyes narrowed until they were slits. Daniel noticed her mouth was now set in a hard line. She looked vicious, primed to strike like an angry cobra. All her experience with Sebastian Pimbleby had made her a fighter, and she had decided no man would disrespect her again.

Two officers strolled past them and nodded. Catherine made to stand up, and one of the gentlemen took her hand and helped her to her feet. Daniel scowled as the men walked to the bow. When they were out of earshot, she turned to him:

"It seems you want to clip my wings just like Sebastian."

Her voice was ice-cold. Each word of her reprimand stung his heart and tightened his throat. Instantly, he regretted his crass comment. His desire to keep her for himself had been thoroughly misunderstood.

"Instead of partying with the sailors and leaving me to fend for myself, you could have

> spent more time in my company. But, considering what you have just implied—don't you dare come near me again. I will assist you with your dig as agreed, and that will be all we do together. When we arrive in Gibraltar, please understand I will not be staying on this ship a moment longer. In place of payment, I believe it is your responsibility to arrange suitable accommodation for me ashore."

He gave the nod in agreement.

With her head held high and her back ramrod straight, she walked towards her cabin. Without her knowledge, her brisk pace made her hips sway naturally from side to side. Daniel did not take his eyes off her. He got the same thrill as when he watched her clear the wall on the Arabian stallion. Except now, he was in even more trouble. Alone, he muttered under his breath, cursing his outburst. *For a man of your maturity and education, Daniel, why do you say the stupidest things?*

Catherine did not speak another word to Daniel until the ship docked in Gibraltar a week later.

As land approached, the towering wall of rock dwarfed the steamship. Catherine stared in awe as the vessel sailed into the picturesque Mediterranean harbour. Noticing her marvelling at her first taste of the area, the captain went over to offer some friendly suggestions.

"Lady Catherine, we will be docking shortly. I recommend that you book into the Bristol Hotel. It is a modern establishment. I have always been comfortable staying there. I imagine that you will need some luxury after enduring a merchant ship. Should you be willing, we can visit the British Consulate, the Governor and his wife are very friendly."

"That will be delightful, captain. It seems a lovely little place to spend some time."

"I will arrange a porter to transfer your luggage to the hotel."

"Thank you, captain, you are most kind."

"You can rely on me. I will ensure that you are well taken care of," he said with a dashing smile.

"Oh, just before you go, captain—one small thing. Can you let the hotel know the professor is to settle the bill for my stay?"

The large elegant reception of the Bristol Hotel in Gibraltar was luxurious. Magnificent oriental rugs lay upon shining mahogany floors. Massive pillars sustained the arches that in turn, supported the vaulted ceiling. Imperious silver chandeliers filling the large domes high above the main entrance. The walls were covered with pale painted wooden panels and embellished with crisp white damask paper, creating a fresh and clean atmosphere. After the cramped and grubby crossing on the merchant vessel, the hotel was a sumptuous indulgence. To her delight, Catherine loved every inch of the place. *The captain certainly knows how to bring a smile to my face.*

Leather sofas and small floral chairs filled the floor area, each carefully positioned grouping accompanied by a white marble table. In the corners, towering palms wafted gracefully, dancing in the cool sea breeze coming in from the open windows and doors. In a large bay window stood a highly polished grand piano, the walnut casing reflecting the lights of a thousand crystals that adorned the chandeliers.

A quartet was playing chamber music in the courtyard. Catherine made her way outside and ordered herself a gin and tonic. It was paradise. As she took a delicious sip, the days of discomfort at sea melted away. She spent the rest of the day relaxing by the pool, engaging in pleasantries with passers-by.

Berthed in the harbour, the ship was surrounded by calm, mirror-like water. Now dark, the full moon high up in the sky, was reflected perfectly on the smooth surface. Daniel was becoming anxious. Catherine was gone all afternoon, and he had no idea where she was, neither it seemed did anyone else.

Finally, he learnt from Captain Grey that Catherine had booked herself into the lavish Bristol Hotel at his suggestion, after telling him she required a little luxury. *A little luxury! The place makes a palace look shabby!*

Daniel was livid she had gone off without even explaining her plans, let alone waiting to see if he approved of her scheme. He bathed and dressed and under the false pretence of going to dinner with the sheikh set out to find her.

Now, Daniel was in two minds as to whether he should stay on the ship or live in the hotel to keep an eye on Catherine. It wasn't an expense he had budgeted for, but he reasoned he could afford it. Alone, he would normally have slept in his cabin. Eventually, he decided he should book a suite. Daniel found that, yet again, Catherine was forcing him to behave out of character. *There are worse ways to be inconvenienced, I suppose. I must admit sounds hotel is impressive, and it will be a pleasure to savour a fine single malt once more and not the sailors' grog.*

Daniel Leicester walked into the Bristol hotel lounge wearing an immaculate black suit, a perfectly pressed white shirt and a dark tie. He carried himself well, and everybody watched the tall black-eyed man command the room's attention with his arrival. He hedged his bets and ordered a scotch, hoping that Catherine Frankland would appear for pre-dinner drinks, rather than choose room service. Having been cooped up for days, he suspected she would prefer to eat in the restaurant.

Catherine's arrival created even more of a stir than Daniel's. He observed that every man in the room had their eyes riveted on her. A hush seized the place for a few seconds. She wore an elegant black gown. It was beaded around the neckline. Her shoulders were smooth and bare. Studded with tiny diamantes on the bodice it sparkled as she moved. Her hair was twisted into an elegant chignon, and she had none of the fussy curls and frills that were so in vogue. The only jewellery that she wore was a pair of pearl earrings. Her grey eyes seemed brighter than usual.

How much did she spend when I said she could get some clothes for the trip! However much it was, love-struck Daniel now felt it was worth every penny.

He stood up and walked towards her. If she felt emotion when she saw him, she was careful not to show it. He could not stop himself smiling. *She looks ravishing.*

> "I trust a little rest and relaxation has been welcome, Lady Frankland?"

Seeing him look so dashing pushed aside the frustration she had felt during their spat on the ship about her mixing with the crew. Further, the afternoon gin and tonics had put her in a more forgiving frame of mind.

Daniel offered her his arm, and she took it graciously. It was the first time that they had touched each other since that fateful night, many years ago at her parent's home. He did not want to let her go, and she wanted to stay on his arm. Unsure of how the scene would play out, neither confessed their true feelings.

"Have you booked into the hotel, Daniel?"

"Yes. I took a suite. It's just a little bit bigger than my onboard cabin. I was in the mood for a little luxury too."

"I highly recommend it," she chirped as she glanced around the palatial bar with a smile.

"May I offer you something to drink, Catherine?"

"Thank you—most kind. I believe the cocktails here are quite something. I would love to try one."

Daniel caught the eye of one of the barmen, and two fancy drinks in exquisite glasses arrived a few minutes later. They sipped their drinks silently as each one battled with their thoughts, wondering how to reveal their romantic feelings. Eventually, a respite from the tension arrived in the form of the sound of the dinner gong.

"Are you ready to eat, yet?" enquired Daniel, seeing an opportunity to push their renewed relationship a little further.

"No, not yet. I am waiting for somebody. He will be here at eight o'clock."

"He?"

"Yes, Captain Grey is escorting me to dinner."

"I will wait with you until he arrives," said Daniel, trying not to look crestfallen.

"Thank you."

"I don't want you to feel awkward when he arrives, Catherine."

"Don't worry. I won't." she reminded him confidently.

That night, Catherine and Daniel dined at separate tables. Captain Grey kept Catherine entertained throughout the whole evening. She giggled and smiled at him, non-stop. *How many hilarious seafaring tales can one man have!* Daniel watched Catherine dazzle the captain with her charm, and he watched Captain Grey acting like a kestrel ready to pounce on a field mouse.

Although Daniel and Catherine still preferred to keep their romantic feelings very much under wraps, neither could keep their eyes off the other—so much so that other guests noticed. Tongues began to wag.

With Gibraltar being such an important military base, it was inevitable some influential people that knew their families would notice the two of them together. Since Catherine had been missing for quite some time, the news was a huge scoop for the gossips that fed the social grapevine—especially since she seemed to be accompanied by one man and making eyes at another. The revelation travelled from the hotel to the British

Embassy. From there, it finally reached the ears of Lady Pimbleby via a friend in London.

"Was she dining with Daniel Leicester?" asked Sebastian.

"No, she was with a certain Captain Grey, the captain of the merchant ship," said his mother.

"Who did she leave with?"

"Lady Delores Muggeridge swears that she was escorted to her bedroom by a man. The porter, who accompanied her in the lift confirmed it."

"Oh, and Leicester, did he sleep at the hotel?"

"Oh, no! No! He went back to the ship. Your wife has taken no visitors since she became a guest there. She has meals in the dining room in full view of the other patrons. It seems she is enjoying the fine weather by sitting on the veranda reading. Although you are not accompanying her, Lady Delores has assured me that she is the epitome of good taste and social grooming."

"Mother, do you think that she is having an affair with Daniel Leicester?"

"Not at all, Sebastian," she reassured him. "I believe that she is on a sabbatical—observing the excavation of the dig site—and that her father has entrusted her in the care of his protégé, Professor Leicester. Finally, we can pinpoint where she is."

"This is better news than I expected, I have to say," confessed Sebastian, clearly relieved.

Lady Pimbleby relaxed for the first time in years. She was well on her way to having a nervous breakdown over Catherine's breach of etiquette. Reuniting her son and daughter-in-law before the opening of the London social season was her primary mission.

Lady Pimbleby knew that from the first time Sebastian had set eyes on Catherine Frankland, a selfish obsession consumed him. Hearing her sons discussing how he deflowered her at a party to blackmail her into marriage, the news of the attack had reached her ears years ago.

However, as much as she despised her son's behaviour, she was delighted that she could get her hands on the Franklands' money. After several bad harvests, the Pimbleby estate was now in dire financial straits. Signs of neglect were everywhere. The mounting debt had to be settled, the dilapidation addressed. Sebastian and Catherine's marriage had been the perfect solution.

Alas, Sebastian Pimbleby had not anticipated that his young naïve wife would be brave enough to leave him. The Frankland family became highly uncooperative. As her husband, he felt Catherine was more a thorn than a rose. Under different circumstances, Lady Pimbleby imagined admiring the young woman's tenacity, rather than find her contemptible.

"Do you know when they will be back in London, mother?"

"A few weeks from now."

"I see," Sebastian made his way towards the door then paused. "Mother, the matter is settled. I will leave for Gibraltar immediately. I'll take Cunard's fastest steamship. I can be there in a few days."

"What an excellent idea," his mother replied encouragingly. "And Sebastian, when you arrive, visit the consulate. Do your best to get you both invited to a formal dinner with the governor. I will ensure that the wonderful news of your attendance reaches the social columns in the Times."

12

THE PICNIC

As time passed, due to his punishing schedule, Daniel and Catherine hardly saw each other. The sheikh had arrived, and they spent the bulk of the day scouring the new chambers at St. Michael's Cave for hints of prehistoric life.

Sheikh Ali Mohammed of Morocco was secretly smitten with Catherine Frankland. She charmed him with her modesty by covering her hair with a hijab, which Daniel thought only emphasised her beautiful features more. The sheikh himself was a prominent archaeologist, widely respected for his discoveries at Timbuktu, the ancient African city. Some evenings, Catherine and the sheikh spent time walking along the seafront, discussing their vastly different cultures and his prestigious career. He was intrigued by her adventures in Arabia and had a great admiration for her father, Sir Herbert.

"My dear," said the handsome sheikh, "archaeology is a brotherhood. We do not care about politics or religion. We take pleasure in our brother's progress. We work toward a common goal, unearthing the past."

"Sheikh Mohammed, I am honoured to hear your opinions."

"Thank you, Lady Frankland, your depth of knowledge has impressed me. As a woman, you are well-educated in the subject."

"That was my father's influence, plus I have read widely. As a child, my family accompanied him on many excavations."

"I believe that British universities accept women these days?"

"Yes, they do," confirmed Catherine demurely.

"Morocco is not an Arab country, Lady Catherine. Our religion is the same, but our culture differs. You must visit and talk with our women. You will be surprised."

"Thank you for the invitation. It will be an honour."

When Daniel overheard one of these conversations, he wished that Catherine was as compliant with him as with the sheikh. *What's his secret to taming her?*

Back in his suite, with Catherine on his mind again, Daniel's brain was a-whirl with thoughts and ideas. It was Saturday tomorrow, perhaps Catherine would accompany him for a walk. There were some small coves and caves that were interesting. *I am sure she will enjoy it. Well, I hope so!*

On tenterhooks, he got dressed for dinner, wondering if at least his outfit would please her, then walked to her room and knocked on the door. He heard her hand touch the door handle.

"Who is it?"

"Daniel," he whispered.

It was quiet for a moment, and then he heard the key turn in the lock.

"Quickly, now! Come in before anybody sees you," she said in a hushed voice.

Stepping into her suite, he noted it was decorated with French antiques and delicate fabrics. A canopied bed dominated the room. Daniel winced when he saw the small sitting area. The impractical rococo furniture was designed for short puny men who never got their hands dirty with hard manual labour.

"I chose this room because it was feminine. I didn't think I needed to take your feelings into consideration."

"I said nothing," he laughed.

"I can read your mind."

"Stop it, Catherine. I didn't come to fight with you."

"Do you want to take off my clothes instead then?"

"I beg your pardon?" he lied, hoping he looked convincing. "Let's go for a picnic tomorrow. I have a little free time at last. There are beautiful caves and beaches—and I know you're bored."

"How?"

"It's quite simple. The captain's conversation is tedious with his endless tales of the sea, and the sheikh is too polite to stray too far from empty small talk."

She laughed. *He has grasped the situation perfectly.*

"Alright. Yes, I will come with you. I feel I need an adventure."

"Excellent. I shall meet you after breakfast," Daniel said with a smile, then slipped out of the room.

Daniel and Catherine set out on the adventure unaccompanied. The hotel kitchen provided a picnic in a knapsack, and they took a cab as far as they could. It was there they began to hike. The sun shone its heavenly warmth on them. When they got onto the soft golden sand, they removed their shoes and walked down the beach looking like two well-dressed shipwreck survivors. Catherine wore a light skirt that settled on her ankles, instead of trailing along the ground. Daniel unbuttoned his shirt a little revealing a little of his muscular chest and rolled his trousers up to his knees. She did her best not to sigh at the glorious sight of him.

Catherine walked along the edge of the water and felt the hard water-soaked sand beneath her feet. At the tip of the cove, the powerful waves crashed into the rugged rock. Daniel walked next to her, basking in the pleasure of the outdoors. There was no confrontation, no angst. At that moment, they were just two people enjoying nature, doing their best to keep their romantic dreams to themselves.

Above a large rocky outcrop, Catherine saw a vast cavern ahead of her.

"Is this where you are working?" she asked.

"Yes, it is."

"What is it called?"

"St. Michael's Cave."

"I thought that it was in Italy."

"Clever girl," he complimented. "This one is named after the Italian cave."

Daniel gave Catherine a tour of the cave, and she was enthralled by it.

"There is another cove a little further on, and we can picnic there," Daniel suggested.

"Yes, I love the idea."

She slipped off her sandals, and Daniel watched her climb barefoot over the rocks, tiptoe along the sand, and make her way to the shore. *There are very few women who would relish in the freedom of the outdoors, but she does—as always.*

The tiny cove had a perfect beach, complete with a small cave of its own. The towering cliffs around it cast some shade to protect them from the harsh midday sunlight. The hotel packed scotch eggs, sandwiches and a bottle of wine. Daniel and Catherine sat in silence as they ate, enjoying the day, the scenery and the peace.

Eventually, Catherine broke the silence.

"Daniel, what am I going to do when I get back to London? I don't see how I can live with you? There is no spare room. Plus, everyone knows Farley and his wife live in the servant's lodgings."

"I am sure there are other lodgings we can arrange. Perhaps rent a spare room from someone nearby. Please forgive me but I don't want to speak about it today. Today, as you might have noticed, is my one free day in ages, and London is far away."

He lay back on the sand and closed his eyes.

"But—," she began.

"I didn't come here to be dragged down pondering problems. I have come here to forget them for a while," he smiled at her. "Come here," he reached out his hand and pulled her toward him, "come lay beside me for a while."

Catherine surprised him. Without hesitation, she lay down—and put her head on his chest. Daniel beamed with delight.

The afternoon was like a dream, they explored the cave. She showed Daniel how to spot fossils in the rock, he explained how he would set out a dig. Eventually, he convinced her to swim with him.

"But I don't have my bathing suit, Daniel?"

"I am sure you'll come up with a solution," he teased.

They undressed and ran into the water like two children, naked, unashamed. It reminded her of the honeymoon in Capri, and her thoughts of Daniel at the Blue Grotto. As they bobbed in the warm sea, she shared the story, and he laughed.

> "So, you were thinking about me, on your honeymoon," he quipped.

She laughed shyly.

> "One day we can swim in the Blue Grotto. I will make it up to you."

Catherine seized her chance.

> "Daniel, do you think we can ever be together?"

The suggestion caught Daniel by surprise, and he struggled to respond. He played it cool.

> "We are together now, Catherine. Just enjoy it, eh?"

When they arrived at the hotel, there was a letter waiting for each of them. Daniel opened his correspondence at the bar over a gin and tonic, whilst Catherine read hers in the cool breeze of the veranda. Curiously, Catherine's note was addressed to Sir and Lady Pimbleby. *The sender is clearly uninformed. I am alone in Gibraltar.* They discovered they were both invited to the British Consulate for dinner at eight o'clock that evening.

Catherine's drink relaxed her, and she felt euphoric. *I could do this forever.* She loved her day with Daniel, He had not tried to seduce her, which was a surprise and a disappointment as he had the perfect opportunity. Navigating their relationship felt like crossing a minefield. Catherine climbed the stairs to the first floor, planning what to wear to dinner with the governor and his wife. The event would be a pleasant end to a perfect day.

Catherine reached her suite and put the key in the lock. She tried to turn it, but it was already open. *Perhaps the maids forgot to lock it?* She pushed the door open and threw her hat onto the bed, she unbuttoned her blouse and removed her skirt. She hummed a tune to herself as she prepared to fling open the wardrobe doors and browsed her array of dresses, wondering which one would be Daniel's favourite.

As she skipped and danced across the room, her eye caught sight a man's jacket hanging on the corner of a chair. *Oh no, I am in the wrong suite!* Then she smelled the stale stench of tobacco. *Definitely the wrong suite!*

In a panic, she darted back to the bed and grabbed her blouse to cover her naked chest. Then with one arm, she fought to put her skirt back on. There was a creak of a chair and some footsteps. A man appeared by the sitting room doorway—it was her husband, Sebastian Pimbleby.

13

THE UNEXPECTED ARRIVAL

"Sebastian!" Catherine choked.

"Catherine, my darling," he stood and looked at her. "You are as beautiful as ever. Don't cover yourself up."

Her eyes were wide and disbelieving. Sebastian was even more unattractive than before, and he repulsed her.

"It has been three years my dear, I have searched all over for you."

"How did you find me?" she snarled.

"Now calm down, Catherine. I thought you would be delighted to see your long lost and devoted husband again."

He laughed menacingly.

"You made the social columns, my dear. The newspaper published that the beautiful Lady Catherine Pimbleby was in Gibraltar on a sabbatical, being entertained by Captain Grey."

"Yes, he was on my ship," she explained, desperate to avoid angering the brute.

"And I believe Professor Leicester is here too."

"Yes, he is working with Sheikh Ali Mohammed from Morocco," she explained, worried that Sebastian seemed to be remarkably well informed about her activities.

"We have been invited to the British Consulate for dinner. Did you receive your invitation?"

"Yes, I did."

"It will be lovely to have you at my side after all these years," Sebastian whispered in her ear.

She could smell the cigar smoke and spirits on his sour breath.

"I am feeling very ill, Sebastian. I think it's the heat. I will have to send them my apologies."

"You seemed fine when you arrived. Brimming with glee even, humming and skipping about the room. Why do that if you were feeling under the weather? Why not immediately rest in bed until you felt better?"

He put his hand out and stroked her fair hair.

"Get dressed, Lady Pimbleby. I am in charge, and you will do as I say."

Catherine trembled with a heady mixture of anger and fear. *What if he tries to overpower me again? The thought sickens me.*

"I brought your lovely sea-green dress. Do you remember it? And those hair combs?"

How could I forget you yanking my dress up as I lay on the ground at that party?

"I know you dressed up just for me that night. Very alluring. Tempting. I expect you to look immaculate—and put on your best wifely performance tonight. Do you hear me?"

"Yes," replied Catherine submissively.

All her bravado was gone. Everything that she had promised herself she would never allow was happening all over again. Catherine felt a depression settle over her. She would have to find a way to survive the night.

Later, at the consulate, Daniel stood in a quiet corner, watching the group of guests. He recognised one or two faces, but no one was familiar enough to talk to. Sheikh Ali Mohammed had gone back to his ship. He had declined the invitation to dinner, fearing the food would not be Halal. It was easier to entertain him in the afternoon over tea and fruit scones.

Regretting agreeing to attend such a formal event, Daniel consoled himself with his welcome drink, a refreshing Kir Royale cocktail. *Hopefully, Catherine will be here soon. At least if I can watch her at a distance, the evening will be tolerable.*

A quartet played some lively classical music in the background which was a welcome distraction. Combined with the excellent whisky, the scene was refined. His skin still felt warm from the afternoon sunshine, and he smiled when he remembered Catherine swimming in the sea with him, the sun-drenched cove, and her joyous laughter. *She has proved herself to be funny, fearless and highly intelligent. I have no doubt I would be happy with her.* He resolved to broach the subject with her the next day. *Seize the day, Daniel. Win her heart once and for all. The practicalities back in London can be dealt with later.*

A glossy black carriage rumbled up the cobbled drive and stopped in front of the consulate building. Sebastian took Catherine's hand to assist her out of the cab. She felt sickened. He escorted her up the steps and into the great hall where forty or so dinner guests mingled, talking in small groups.

As they entered the impressive mansion, Sebastian and Catherine were formally introduced to the governor and his wife. They were both dazzled by Catherine's graceful charm. A waiter offered them two cocktails from an exquisite silver tray. Sebastian grabbed his wife's elbow as he steered her in front of the throng where the butler officially announced their arrival.

"Sir Sebastian and Lady Catherine Pimbleby."

At the sound of Catherine's name, Daniel Leicester spun around. He was revolted by what he saw. *What is he doing here?* He noticed Sebastian touching the small of her back while he escorted her. She showed no sign of resistance. Daniel's jaw clenched so tightly his next mouthful of soothing scotch would have to wait.

A hush fell over the small crowd as they watched the elegant young woman process across the room, with grace and confidence. Her turquoise dress was magnificent, and her hair pinned up with the most beautiful Japanese combs. Her proud smile lit up the room. Politely, the couple greeted some of the groups of guests.

Daniel was confused and devastated. His mood changed in an instant. *She cannot be giving him a second chance, can she? It seems she is happy to submit to the whims of polite society after all. But why? It's like I hardly know her.*

He could not stand to look at either of them and went off to find a waiter and ordered another drink. He was filled with an overwhelming rage for Catherine. *Why must she forever blow hot and cold? I am sick of it. If she wants Pimbleby, she is welcome to him!* Before he lost his temper in front of everybody, he planned to have one last drink, then excuse himself saying there was urgent matter back at the ship.

Catherine saw Daniel leaning against the wall at the back of the room and looked straight into his eyes. Her smile never waned. Neither did she show an ounce of fear or regret. She seemed to have command of the room. Sebastian Pimbleby held her arm while they walked from guest to guest introducing themselves, sticking to her like glue. Heartbroken, Daniel swallowed his final dregs of whisky in one mouthful and replaced the crystal tumbler on the waiter's tray.

With his head held high and every eye upon him, he spoke briefly to the governor, then left the party. Catherine watched him from the corner of her eye. She thought of them naked in the idyllic Mediterranean cove. *What a magical day it was. Perfect even.* Her heart wanted to break too. If only she could explain that Sebastian had threatened her, forced her to dazzle the Governor, or there would be hell to pay back at the hotel. *There is no chance of that happening now.* For a moment, Catherine's cheerful mask slipped, and she bit her lip anxiously. The ever-watchful Sebastian dug his fingers into her elbow that little bit deeper until her mouth was upturned once more.

In the humid evening air, Daniel undid his top button and loosened his tie as he stomped across the town, searching for a pub where he could get as drunk as a sailor. The word 'entertainment' caught his eye. He pushed his way through the doors of the establishment and into a hot and crowded pub. There was a small stage at the far end with a sign advertising tonight's star act, Miss Evelyn Edwards, 'the Welsh Nightingale'.

After spending some time elbowing his way to the bar, Daniel erred on the side of caution and ordered three drinks. The barman stacked them in a row.

"Is it that bad, mate?"

"Mind your own business," growled Daniel.

"Don't worry, guv. You've seen there's a good show coming up soon, yeah? That'll cheer you up."

"Mmm."

Daniel wished that the barman would stop being so damned jolly.

He looked at the men around him, most were dockers or sailors. They were a rowdy bunch. Although very over-dressed in comparison, Daniel felt comfortable in their company—it was honest. A few of them were so drunk, they could be written off for the night. Others stood about singing and joking. The remainder, like Daniel, watched the comings and goings of the rabble.

There was a flurry of notes from the piano, and all eyes turned to the small stage. A man, quite possibly the owner, stood up and made an announcement.

> "Gentlemen," he shouted, "there is only one lady in the room tonight."

The men cheered and whistled.

> "The lady with the golden voice, the Welsh nightingale—" The men roared in appreciation. "—Miss Evelyn Edwards!"

The piano began to play, and a short woman aged about thirty waltzed onto the stage. She had blonde curls hanging to her shoulders and huge blue eyes and a mouth adorned with scarlet lipstick. She looked like a doll. As her trademark stage costume, over the years it had proven to be excellent at getting everyone's attention.

She was a buxom woman with an hourglass figure. She chose a revealing dress that excelled at showcasing it. The neckline plunged, and her hemline ended a good eight inches above her knees. The sight of her womanly flesh raised a gasp and whoop from the sailors. Her voice, as sweet as a songbird, delivered songs laden with suggestion but not so much that they were crass. Daniel was surprised that he enjoyed the bawdiness of her act before he decided he loved it.

The time had passed in a flash. As quickly as the Welsh nightingale had arrived, she left. Without the pleasant distraction, Daniel's mind flitted back to the subject of Catherine. Now, with several drinks down the shoot, his stubborn resentment and recklessness came to the fore. *If Catherine thinks it is acceptable to spend the night in bed with someone she hates, I will find somebody that I can enjoy. For all her talk of hating Sebastian, she capitulated rather quickly. Perhaps, she is not as unconventional as she made out?*

"Where does Miss Edwards live?" enquired Daniel.

"So, she did cheer you up then?"

"I asked for her address, please, my good man."

"She's a singer, guv, not a wench."

Daniel threw some banknotes across the countertop. The barman picked them up and put it in his pocket.

"We call her Evie, guv. Go up the street and turn left. There's a small boarding house on the corner. She'll be there."

"Husband?"

"No, guv, she's far too smart for that."

Daniel got to the boarding house and opened the door into the hallway. He was slightly off-balance from drink but did his best to be presentable. Then, Daniel got a fright that almost sobered him.

"Who are you looking for, mister?" said a male voice out of the darkness.

"I'm looking for Evie," he replied.

"Everyone is looking for Evie, mate. Go home, she ain't that kinda gal."

Daniel wasn't going to be turned away that easily.

"I asked you to call for her."

"No!" answered the man. "It's the drink talking, fella. Get outta here before I fetch the bobby."

"To hell with you and your petty little rules."

Daniel began to yell at the top of his voice.

"Evie! Evie! Come down here. I am looking for you."

By this time, most of the tenants had opened their doors and watched the dishevelled-looking man in the posh suit with amusement.

"Eeevieee!" he yelled.

She came bounding down the stairs.

"Oh, dear God, who is making that racket?"

"Do ye know him, lass?" asked the man at the desk.

Evie looked at Daniel, and an old instinct told her he was harmless. In his suit, he looked like he had a few bob too, not a typical sailor type.

"Yea, I know him. It's alright."

Daniel followed her up the stairs to her room, a small clean space. A kettle on the small fireplace made it homely. Lacking a wardrobe, various revealing costumes and a collection of wigs adorned the furniture. He could see her stockings hanging up tantalisingly in the bathroom.

Daniel collapsed into a chair.

"Right! What's yer name? And what's with making a bloody commotion an' all at this time of night."

"Daniel. And I was looking for you."

"Right! Well, let me tell yer something, Mister Daniel. I don't want to lie te yer like, but you going to get me into a lot of hot water, hollering like that."

"Come here, Evie," he said, pulling her onto his lap.

In her career, Evie had experience with many a heckling drunk. Daniel was going to be one of the easy ones to manage. She loosened his tie and undid his top button then struck up a conversation to buy her some time.

"Now, what is a handsome well-to-do bloke like you doing here like?" she asked in a sing-song voice.

He put his hand on her knee to test the water. *She didn't push me away. That's a good sign.*

"Oh, Evie, I don't know where to start."

"Right, Daniel, let me start for you: you are in love, my pet. Just start there?"

"Yes, I—am," he hiccupped.

"Yeah, mate, I know. And she don't love you?"

"No, she has gone back to her husband, the man is a filthy pig farmer. Mean too. 'A nasty piece of work' as you might say."

"Oh, right," said Evie. "That is a disaster. The bad men always seem to be able to attract the pretty ones."

At the mention of the word pretty, it was dawning on Evie how alluring Daniel was.

"I have never loved any other woman as I do her," he lamented. Feeling even more woozy and angry, his voice became more of a yell. "I've half a mind to find the fellow and bash his brains in. Swooping in and taking her from me like that. Teach him some manners."

Somewhat panicked, Evie clapped her hand over his mouth.

"No more of that sort of talk, Daniel. If something happens to that man, you will be locked up in no time. Keep yer trap shut, alright?"

"Right!" said Daniel. He bit his bottom lip before whispering, "I can think of another way to stop me shouting."

He tilted his head towards her and kissed her. She put up no resistance. Gently, he glided her off his lap and stood up.

"Come, Evie," he nagged, tugging her arm.

"I'm not one of 'em girls, Daniel. I am a singer."

"Yeah, but I am one of those blokes. How much can I pay you to fall in love with me for one night?"

Evie looked him up and down. Compared to the coarse sailors who were always propositioning her, it wouldn't be impossible to fall in love with a handsome man for a few hours—especially if the price was right. It wasn't like she was awash with cash. He fumbled in his pocket and pulled out the last of his money.

"Is this enough?" he asked.

Taking her broad grin to mean yes, he pulled her onto the bed gently.

"What's her name, this girl of yours?" Evie asked tenderly.

"Catherine. And I love her. Just like I love you—for tonight at least."

She smiled, won over by his honesty.

"I think you need to have a heart-to-heart with Catherine. Tell her how you feel."

He tried to undress, fighting to remove his tie. His trousers proved to be a challenge, so he let them bunch up around his knees.

"I've tried, God knows I've tried. I want to marry her. Always have," he muttered.

He tried to roll on top of Evie, but the drink was robbing him of his coordination. He felt like a deadweight. With a gentle shove, he soon slid down beside her.

He lay his head on her chest. "You are so beautiful, Catherine," he whispered as his heavy-lidded eyes began to flicker closed. "He won't love you like I love you."

> "I know, Daniel, I know," she said, stroking his hair. "It'll all work out in the end, you mark my words, my flower."

Evie felt his body relax and fall into a deep sleep. His shirt was unbuttoned, and his trousers still around his knees. She carefully moved away and covered him with a blanket. Her job was done. He had his answer. All he needed was to speak to somebody and unburden his soul. The problem had been shared and halved.

A startled Daniel woke up, semi-dressed in the early hours of the morning. He reached down and was relieved to find his underwear was still on. He glanced over at the fully dressed Evie, asleep in the chair, relieved that he hadn't been able to perform in his drunken state.

He tidied up his clothing and crept towards the door. He turned back to look at her and smiled in gratitude. *You're a clever girl. Cleverer than me.* He snuck out of the boarding house and hoped to make it back to the hotel without being seen.

Daniel got to the Bristol Hotel dishevelled but sober. He took the stairs to the first floor. When he saw Catherine's suite, a terrible crushing melancholy took hold of him. As he tiptoed past her door, he heard a muffled cry. He stopped. Pressing his ear gently to the door, he heard Pimbleby's menacing voice.

"I told you to do it, you whore! Do you remember your vows— to love, honour and obey?"

"Stop it, Sebastian! No! Don't!"

"I bet you have whored with all and sundry over the past three years. Now you can service me," he snarled.

"You are hurting me! Stop!"

Daniel heard a loud slap, and then silence. Desperate to know more, he tried pressing his other ear to the door. It was then he heard Catherine begin to cry.

Hearing the abuse, Daniel rested his forehead against the doorpost, his heart broken yet again, and his dreams shattered. He wanted to weep, but he knew it would paralyse him if he let his emotions run wild. Meddling in another man's marriage was not the way he saw his love life panning out.

Pimbleby began screaming obscenities again, and Catherine continued to beg for mercy. There was another loud thump, sounding like a fist hitting soft flesh.

Daniel tried the handle of the door, but it was locked. Animal instinct took over, and he gave the door a swift kick. The lock splintered. The door swung open. A nude Sebastian stood in front of a naked Catherine, who was cowering on her knees. He was pulling her by her hair, trying to manoeuvre her toward his groin. When he saw Daniel, he pushed Catherine roughly aside. The force made her topple over.

"Catherine, get up."

She looked up at him, terrified, frozen in fear.

"I said, get up and get dressed."

She lunged at her robe draped over the edge of the bed, then fled to the bathroom, locking the door behind her.

"What are you doing, Leicester? You can't barge in here and order my wife about."

Daniel was undeterred. Sebastian looked apoplectic, his temple veins pulsing with rage.

"Are you dressed, Catherine?" Daniel asked reassuringly.

"Yes."

"Good. Now, I want you to open the door."

The bolt slid back, and the door opened very slightly. A single petrified eye peered out into the room. He took a large headscarf from the dressing table and passed it to her through the gap.

Sebastian, stunned by Daniel's rudeness and slowed by a night of heavy drinking, was rooted to the spot.

"Put that over your head and go downstairs, as quickly and quietly as you can, then wait for me."

At that suggestion, Sebastian began to protest.

"Don't you dare listen to him, Catherine. Don't you dare. I will give you the beating of your life. God knows you deserve it if you choose to desert me again."

Catherine made for the door angering Sebastian further stills. He became even more menacing.

"You remember I shot your horse in the head? I'll come after you and your family if you shame mine any more with this reckless behaviour of yours."

By now, Sebastian was shouting like a madman.

Just before she left the room, Catherine looked at Daniel for support.

"Go, Catherine. I will look after you. In the meantime, you will be safer downstairs," said Daniel calmly.

"You can't do this. It is adultery," the naked Sebastian screamed and cursed, "I will find you and kill you."

Catherine fled. Several guests were standing on the landing, woken by the almighty row. She pushed through them, wishing the earth would swallow her up.

Sebastian's ranting filled the air, with Daniel trying to reason with him as he stuffed Catherine's belongings into her suitcase. He also sneaked Sebastian's trousers into the case to slow his pursuit.

Less than a minute later, Daniel walked out of Catherine's suite, leaving the door open for the inquisitive crowd to see how insane Sebastian Pimbleby really was. The onlookers had all heard the threats and the accusations. They had seen a bruised and battered Catherine Pimbleby escape from her cruel husband, with Daniel acting in her defence.

In a flash, he collected his few belongings and dashed downstairs. As soon as she saw Daniel, Catherine lost her composure.

"He is going to murder me. I know it!" she cried hysterically.

"No, he's not. I'll see to that."

"He is going to murder my family. He shot my horse, my beautiful Arabian stallion."

"I won't let him," he said soothingly as he put a comforting arm around her.

When her sobbing abated, Daniel stood up and offered her his hand.

> "Where are you taking me? Not back to him! Please!" she asked, her grey eyes red and puffy both from the tears and the beating she sustained at the hands of her husband.

> "Back to the ship," he smiled. "We are going home."

Catherine had never heard a better suggestion in her life. They sailed a few hours later, at daybreak. Daniel could not settle until the ship was out of the harbour, and they were well out of the reach of Sebastian. When he was finally at peace, just before breakfast, he went to Catherine's cabin.

He enfolded her in his arms and stroked her hair.

> "I am terribly concerned about you abandoning the dig," she confessed.

> "Don't you worry about that. I can come back. They are prehistoric objects we're looking for. They can stay buried a little longer," he reassured.

> "But what will the university say?"

> "The sheikh will take care of it. I left him a letter."

"You have left everything that matters to you behind."

"No, I haven't," he said with a smile. "You are with me."

As always, Catherine, despite her humiliating ordeal was strong and resilient. She refused to wallow in self-pity nor sink into a depression. It was Daniel that couldn't get the picture of Pimbleby out of his mind. *I have not finished with that man yet.*

During the long return sailing, Daniel spent hours with Catherine, reading and teaching her about his archaeological work. She was hungry for knowledge, and he realised she would make a perfect researcher. She questioned everything and did not stop referencing and cross-referencing until she was satisfied that the information was correct.

A protective Daniel escorted her around the ship, accompanied her to meals, and they spent splendid nights sitting on the deck together, watching the stars move across the cloudless night sky.

One such picturesque night, he escorted her downstairs. He finally made love to her with a tenderness that she had never experienced in all her married years.

On the open sea, they were safe, far away from critical stares and insatiable gossips. Still, Daniel knew that once they got to London, things would be difficult. News of what happened at the suite would already have reached the capital. The social pages would be eager to report the scandal, particularly Catherine Pimbleby (née Frankland) leaving the Bristol Hotel with Professor Daniel Leicester.

13

THE MOTHER'S DISAPPOINTMENT

"Your wife is now living in sin with Daniel Leicester, and you have made yourself the laughing stock of England," Lady Pimbleby hissed.

"Mother, you cannot believe what she put me through! She tormented and humiliated me until I lost my temper," he said in his defence.

"Unfortunately, I find that explanation very hard to believe. I gave you clear instructions to charm Catherine back into your life. Instead, your cruel and jealous streak drove you to lose your mind in front of all the hotel guests, not to mention your state of undress when you did it," she sneered at him. "If it weren't for the governor being an acquaintance, you would have been put in gaol."

"Daniel Leicester dared to kick down the door while we were having a perfectly private moment."

"I heard tales that her cries were coming from that room for hours. Lady Delores reported that he behaved like a gentleman and didn't touch you. Daniel Leicester is now considered a hero, and you the villain of the piece."

"You know how dramatic Catherine is. I will fetch her and take her to our London house, and you can deal with her," said Sebastian. "I am sure you will be more measured in your handling of the situation."

"I will not be going anywhere near London. I am the laughing stock of the season."

"Mother, we can still make amends."

"No, we cannot. Thanks to your foolish and crass antics in Gibraltar, you have ruined what was left of my reputation. I have a good mind to cede this estate to the crown when I die."

"What do you mean?"

"The crown is capable of running it, not like you, who seem to be hell-bent on ruining it."

Sebastian left his mother in absolute humiliation. He regretted the day that he had set eyes on Catherine Frankland. He was happy to give her a home, provide servants for her. All he wanted was his physical needs fulfilled by his wife, and to provide an heir. *I spent months trying to impregnate her. It was clear that she was doing something to prevent it. Things should have been so simple, but they never were.*

Sebastian reasoned like a mad man. Hatred and jealousy saturated his mind, and he could think of nothing else but vengeance. I *shall kill that menace of a man. I am sure he can tumble down one of those deep excavations of his. Then, perhaps, Catherine will finally accept me as her husband—til death us do part.*

In London, Dianna Hamilton-Gordon was at her father's side, sauntering through Hyde Park. She was the epitome of a lady, immaculately groomed, demure and beautiful. A prime example of courtesy and grace, everybody who met her was impressed.

Wives would comment to their husbands that they 'should invite the Hamilton-Gordon's for dinner,' or perhaps introduce her to their sons. Husbands would nod in agreement, commenting on Sir Rufus' fine parenting skills, to have raised such a virtuous daughter after the death of his beloved wife. The cold and scheming streak she inherited from her father seemed to go miraculously unnoticed.

"My dear, Dianna," Sir Rufus said, "I have heard that Daniel Leicester has returned from Gibraltar."

"Yes, father. The news has reached everybody."

"I believe Catherine Pimbleby is living in his apartment. He says she is helping him as a researcher. I don't believe a word of it—utter tosh. You can't swing a cat in that place of his, it's so small. I think we can all guess what that means about their sleeping arrangements."

"Yes, father, it is such a scandal. All of London is gossiping about it. I imagine that Sir James must be at his wits' end."

"He will not tolerate this rogue behaviour from his son, believe me. If I were him, I'd do everything in my power to contain the damage Daniel has caused. I have noticed their invites to future society events have dried up completely. Now, he will have more of an appetite to put pressure on his rebellious son. I just hope that Daniel Leicester has not passed the point of no return."

"Father, do I really have to remind you that men usually walk away from scandals with a flawless reputation? This debacle will destroy

Catherine, not him. She will never survive it. It will be amusing to watch her retreat to a little coastal village in Scotland somewhere. Not even a fisherman will want to marry her."

"You're right, Dianna. I am sure we can resolve this little matter together."

"Do you feel sorry for Sir Herbert Frankland, having such a wicked and ungrateful daughter?" asked Dianna.

"Never," replied Sir Rufus. "The man has been a thorn in my side for years, opposing my views in parliament more times than I care to remember."

He paused to take a sip of his drink.

"So, are we in agreement that you will approach Daniel Leicester this week?" said Sir Rufus, his beady little eyes dancing in delight.

"Of course, father. You can count on it."

Sir James Leicester summoned Daniel to his Pall Mall club. A reluctant Daniel had to don formalwear to gain admission to the exclusive venue. He dressed smartly in an understated black suit. He strode into the bar, unintimidated by the men around him, and cast his eye about, looking for his father. Daniel spotted him in a far corner and carefully manoeuvred his way through the groups of men in deep discussion. Sir James greeted him as he sat down on the neighbouring winged chair.

"I wasn't sure if you would come," grunted Sir James.

"Neither was I."

"Do you have to be so damned difficult?"

"If you are going to lecture me about Catherine Frankland, the answers are, 'no' and 'no'."

"Whatever do you mean?" said his father with a frown.

"No, I am not telling Catherine to leave. And, no, I am not marrying Dianna Hamilton-Gordon."

"Daniel, why are you intent on making such a blunder?"

"It is not a blunder, father. It is a choice. A conscious, well-considered choice."

"You are choosing to live with a scarlet woman, here in the middle of London, under everyone's watchful gaze and still believe you can be accepted?"

"No, father. Quite the opposite. But I am prepared for the backlash, and I will not leave Catherine's side."

"It's more than 'backlash', Daniel," his father warned. "Sebastian Pimbleby has every right to sue you for adultery."

"I hope that he does," said Daniel contemptuously.

"Good God. Don't you see? You are jeopardising our estate. We could end up with nothing."

"The only reason Catherine Frankland married Pimbleby was that she was raped and blackmailed by him. Are you suggesting that his behaviour towards her has been acceptable?"

Sir James dismissed the information with an arrogant wave of his hand.

"I found her on her knees in front of the brute, sobbing, begging him to stop beating her."

"These little tiffs arise between married people. Besides she abandoned him for three years, what did she expect? To be welcomed with a red carpet? I would have done the same thing. She needed to be put in her place."

"She has suffered more humiliation than a person should. I will protect her from the hypocrisy of the whole sorry system that this country calls 'justice.'"

"Your talk is dangerous, Daniel. Especially in this club."

"You have disappointed me, father."

"And you me, Daniel."

"I have made my choice, and I choose Catherine to be my wife. If we cannot marry in this country, we will marry somewhere else."

With that, he was gone, leaving a simmering Sir James to his anguish about what would happen next.

Sebastian Pimbleby travelled to London by train and headed to his mother's small apartment in Kensington. Wisely, he decided to choose somewhere as low-key as possible, dreading the idea that the press would announce his arrival in London if he picked a West End hotel.

He dismissed half of the staff, and the other half were threatened with their jobs if they dared disclose his whereabouts. Sebastian spent two whole weeks, working late into the evening, plotting his course of action against his troublesome wife. Revenge was to be sweet.

After one final late night, he went to bed with an evil smile, delighted with his cunning solution. Finally, he would wield power over his errant wife. This time, he made sure his plan was foolproof, engineering it so that he needed no direct involvement. *This time, I shall hire somebody else to do my dirty work.*

Sebastian awoke, washed, shaved and donned a fresh suit. At breakfast, he was unusually cheerful. Fed and watered, it was time to invoke his grand scheme.

"Wapping," he barked at his driver.

"Yes, sir."

Sebastian's cab stopped in front of the Pig & Whistle. The pub was much the same as any other dockside pub. It was grubby and filled with rough lower-class men and a few loud women. It was very early, but that did not deter the dockhands from drinking after their night shift. Sebastian walked up to the bar, acting like royalty.

"I am looking for Ogilvy."

"Mmm, he's out supervising a load. I will send somebody to fetch him."

Sebastian mumbled an uncharacteristic 'thank you'.

"Can I get you an ale while yer wait, guv?"

"Yes," answered Sebastian. "Why not?"

It took about thirty minutes for Ogilvy to appear. By that time, Sebastian had drunk two more pints. Now, he was full of Dutch courage. Ogilvy walked over to where Sebastian was sitting.

"Sebastian," said Ogilvy, reaching out to shake the man's hand.

"Good morning," he said with a smile. "You are at the old grindstone early today."

"No rest for the wicked is there now?" Ogilvy chuckled.

"I suppose not."

"I believe you raised hell in Gibraltar," said Ogilvy with a wry smile.

Sebastian sniffed in a deep breath as he thought of a suitable response.

"Well, of course, everything is misrepresented in the press. All a lie."

"Of course," agreed Ogilvy, knowing how to play the likes of Sebastian.

"This whole rumpus has been rather unsettling for me, and it is not good for mother or the estate. You cannot imagine the social repercussions of my wayward wife's behaviour."

"Do you think there is anything I can do to help you?" asked Ogilvy sombrely. "I will assist you in any way I can, old chap. We go back a long way, don't we? She needs to be taught who rules the roost in your household."

"Yes, yes!" exclaimed Sebastian. "You read my mind. She is living with Daniel Leicester in Mayfair."

"She's still with him?" Ogilvy said, shaking his head.

"I want her kidnapped and brought to me."

"Hmm. That might be tricky."

"How so?" asked Sebastian.

"Well, you need experienced professionals to do a proper job. You don't want some fresh-faced chancer messing it up, especially if they get their collars felt by the plod. If you have the money, I can find the right people to help you," Ogilvy said shrewdly.

"It will be priceless to see her beg for mercy. Once the matter of my wife is dealt with, we will take care of Daniel Leicester," plotted Sebastian.

"Yes, maybe for a little more they can—you know—soften her up a little? Tame her wild side."

"Yes, I like that idea. I want her afraid—too afraid to refuse me again in her wifely duties."

Ogilvy raised his eyebrows, eager for Pimbleby to elaborate, but he chose not to.

"I'll make some enquiries. Meet me here tomorrow, and I will bring my cronies."

The two men shook hands and bid each other farewell. Ogilvy watched Sebastian walk away. *If I were a woman, I wouldn't want to touch him either—but money's money.* He cracked his knuckles. *This sounds like a lucrative little job.*

Ogilvy took a slow walk to Seven Dials. Despite his bulk, he enjoyed a stroll from time to time. It gave him some quiet time to think away from the shouting and clanking at the dockside. He hadn't set up a job this important for years, and it got the old juices flowing. It gave him a certain thrill, even if secretly, he felt it was Sebastian who was at fault. Eventually, he saw the barbershop that he was looking for and went in.

A bell tinkled as he closed the door behind him. A kindly looking man turned around from his customer and recognised Ogilvy instantly.

"Can I go through?" he asked.

The barber nodded.

Ogilvy took the stairs to the first floor and found a door guarded by two thuggish men.

"I want to speak to Dougie Simpson," he said importantly.

The two brutes didn't acknowledge Ogilvy's request at all, apart from smirking in unison. After watching their visitor squirm with helplessness for a moment or two, they knocked on the door and announced his arrival to their boss.

"Ogilvy, me old mucker!" greeted the strong cockney accent.

"It has been a long time, Dougie. Too long. How's business?"

"Oh, you know. Up and down. Had a few brushes with the law, but nothing me and the lads couldn't handle. A bit of witness intimidation goes a long way. While you're here, do you want a small nip of sumfink?"

"Of course, you know me, Dougie."

"So, is this a business call?"

"Oh, yes. Most definitely. Now, listen to this. A friend of mine is having a spot of bother with his wife. Bold as brass, she's gone and upped sticks to shack up with another man! He needs her nicked out of her lover's apartment in Mayfair and roughed up a bit. Show her the error of her ways. A nice simple little job. Perhaps something for your boys to enjoy before they hand her over," Ogilvy laughed.

"Mmm," answered Dougie.

"Of course, the purse is large. My friend is keen to bring the matter to a close. It has been rumbling along for far too long. He wants to get his marriage back on track—at least to onlookers."

"Blimey, Ogilvy! Right, we need to understand each other on this matter. We will nick her, alright. She may get a wallop here and there if she is difficult—but we don't violate women. We are businessmen first and foremost. It's the cold hard cash we're interested in, not 'perks'."

"As you wish. I will have my friend at the Pig and Whistle tomorrow at midday. Alright?"

"I need not remind you that kidnapping is a step up from our previous arrangements, Ogilvy."

"Yes, I appreciate that."

"It had better be worth the trouble—or I may break your arm for wasting me time," said Dougie with a wink.

The wink didn't soothe Ogilvy's nerves in the slightest. It was an out-and-out threat. Dougie Simpson was a ruthless man.

13

A STRING OF MEETINGS

Daniel ran up the stairs to the rooms of the barrister, John Cowie. He and Daniel had been friends for many years, since their university days, and he trusted John's legal abilities.

John was delighted to see his pal, and they fell into a comfortable conversation about days gone by. Inevitably, the conversation turned to more pressing matters.

> "To be honest, Daniel, I expected you to be here sooner. The city is on fire with talk of you and Catherine Frankland, sorry Lady Pimbleby."
>
> "I know," answered Daniel, "but I will not see her forced back to that monster."
>
> "At some point, Sebastian is going to sue you for adultery," advised John.

"Perhaps, he will. However, I am here to discuss another matter."

"I hope it isn't as controversial as Catherine—"

"—It's worse," interrupted Daniel with a laugh.

"Worse?" mouthed John, as his eyes widened in disbelief.

"Go on."

"I want to waive my inheritance to the Leicester estate. Let my brothers have it."

John sat back and looked at him, earnestly.

"Do you understand the implication of that decision?"

"Of course, I do. I will be poor," Daniel laughed nervously.

"And," said John, "your paternity is going to be questioned."

"I think my father often questions it already. We are very different."

Daniel smirked. John looked on, concerned.

"What has led to this decision?"

"People think wealth is the be-all and end-all to a happy life. For me, it is a noose. My every move is scrutinised. Tongues wag every time I do something for myself rather than what I 'should' be doing as a member of polite society. I have had enough. It's time for me to cut myself free from it."

"Can you support yourself, Daniel?"

"Yes, I have supported myself for years. I own my property. My job at the university is well paid. I have never requested a penny from my father since I graduated. I will not be a wealthy man, but I will be a happy man."

"And Catherine—Lady Frankland as was—will she be satisfied to live a middle-class life?"

"Given that when she ran away from Sebastian, she was happy to live in a squalid Whitechapel tenement, struggling to keep her head above water, what I can provide will be more than adequate. Besides, we want peace, and we want each other."

"There are various progeniture laws to be considered, but we will contact your father's counsel and discuss it with him. It's rare of course, but you are not the first nor the last person who has chosen to waive his inheritance. I will support you in your decision."

Daniel finally felt he was taking charge of his future. The two men shook hands and promised to see each other soon.

Back in Wapping, a fidgety Sebastian Pimbleby sat in the Pig and Whistle, filled with excitement at the thought of meeting someone who could actually tame that headstrong wife of his.

In a sign of deference, Ogilvy opened the pub door, and the mobster walked in ahead of him. Dougie was a man in his early fifties, neat as a pin and infamous in the areas of Whitechapel and Spitalfields, who ran the dockside in Wapping. Sebastian noticed men begin to leave one by one as soon as Dougie Simpson walked in—the ones who owed him money.

Dougie opened the conversation.

"I don't often meet my clients face to face. Usually, I send one of my men. But you are a big name. You are lucky I have taken the time to see you," he said arrogantly.

Sebastian's blood pressure rapidly rose at the man's insolence.

"I am the client, so learn some manners."

"Now, now gentlemen," intervened Ogilvy, not wanting to lose the opportunity of making some extra cash. "Tensions are obviously running high. Let's start again, shall we?"

Both the men nodded.

"Do you have an address for me?" asked Dougie.

Sebastian passed him a card with the details.

"She is living with a man called Daniel Leicester. He's a professor at the university."

"We will have to watch the residence for a few days before we take action. Make sure we can get the job done cleanly. No snags," advised Dougie, "Surveillance is going to cost you quite a bit of money."

"Whatever it takes, Mr Simpson. Before I pay you, I trust you have done this type of job before?"

Ogilvy winced at Sebastian's audacity.

"Shut yer gob, posh boy, or I'll put me fist right down yer pie hole."

"Fine. Calm down. How much will it cost?"

"A thousand quid should cover it."

"What!" Sebastian exclaimed.

"You need me more than I need you. Five hundred quid up front, the rest on receipt of the goods. Ogilvy will collect the first instalment from you tomorrow. You pay my boys when they bring her to you. Agreed? Where do we deliver her to?" asked Dougie.

"My house in Kensington."

"I will work through Ogilvy. I never want to see you again, Pimbleby."

"Will she be more compliant when she is delivered?" enquired Sebastian.

"Possibly," answered Dougie. "We are only kidnappers, remember, not ringmasters taming a lion."

"Then I want a discount," snarled Sebastian, slammed his fist on the table.

"Listen to me, mate," Dougie hissed through gritted teeth, "you toffs are used to giving the orders. You made a right mess when you tried to throw your weight around in Gibraltar. You don't want to know what I will do to you if you open yer gob again. It's time for you to show a guy like me some respect for once in yer life, pal. I ain't too fond of your tone. Understand?"

Moments later Dougie was gone, storming out in a furious temper. Sebastian was now speechless, dazed by the encounter. He had never met a common man who dared to be so rude to him, but he decided to tolerate it, mainly because he had no other options.

Ogilvy looked at him and spoke harshly.

> "From now on, I will handle the business side of things, Sebastian. If I leave it to you, you will get us both killed."

Sebastian nodded his head. He had finally met his nemesis in Dougie Simpson, and he was terrified. His mother's verbal attacks paled into insignificance.

Arthur Champley, Sir James Leicester's lawyer, travelled to the family estate, preferring to speak directly to his client.

> "What?" roared Sir James. "He wants to do what?"

> "He wants to relinquish his inheritance," repeated Arthur Champley with a sigh.

Arthur's whole career had been built on people fighting for more money, and here he had a case of the opposite. It was a refreshing professional challenge, but he thought it best to keep that to himself.

> "All my other sons are married already," yelled Sir James Leicester.

"You may leave it to the second eldest, sir."

"That is not the point. With no dowry, I will lose a fortune if Daniel makes this choice."

"We cannot make it a legal matter to force him to comply, Sir James. We will be laughed right out of the court, and be the laughing stock of Westminster."

"Is there anything that we can do to put an end to this matter before it becomes public knowledge?"

"No, sir, nothing."

16

TOGETHER—FOR NOW

Catherine and Daniel lay naked under the canopy of the large ebony bed. She was still fast asleep. Her one arm was stretched across his broad chest, and her leg lay over him. Daniel had been awake for some time but did not have the will to move her. He felt her warm body against him, and all that he desired was to peel back the sheet and make love to her. He smiled at the idea.

Her long curly hair was tousled, and Daniel gently played with a lock as he watched her slow and steady breathing. He couldn't help himself any longer, and he put his hand under the sheet and stroked the top of her thigh. Catherine sighed and smiled. She opened her eyes drowsily and saw him gazing down at her. He looked beautiful in the morning. He raised himself onto his elbow, and Catherine rolled onto her back. He lowered his head and kissed her gently as his hands took in every curve. Catherine made it clear she wanted him to go further.

In no time at all, they had settled into a simple routine. Their days were filled with intellectual pastimes, and their nights were filled with passion. When Daniel was not at the university, he was researching several projects at home. By now, Catherine was able to assist him with a range of subject matter. He suggested she catalogue his books and papers, many of them still filed in piles on the floor. Now, she knew which pile to search if Daniel requested a particular text or folder.

Daniel also invested in a typewriter and instructed her to learn how to use it. When he was lecturing, Mr Farley could hear her slow clack-clacking while she practised. In the evenings, they lay in front of the fireplace, talking, and eventually, they found their way to bed.

Although their life was peaceful at home, Daniel was inundated with criticism at the university. The situation between him and Catherine had reached the faculty dean's ears, who considered the relationship scandalous and told Daniel so.

"Javier, my private life is becoming a political issue within the university," said a frustrated Daniel.

"I understand. In Spain, the church would excommunicate me."

"Is it important for you to follow their rules?"

"Yes, my family would disown me, and I don't know if any woman would have me if I was excluded from the Catholic faith."

"Catherine and I will never have peace until we move out of London. She has not left the apartment since we have returned from Gibraltar. She lives life like a prisoner. Everyone has sided with Sebastian. They have conveniently forgotten his brutal treatment of her. Her only friend is a prostitute in Whitechapel—and she doesn't even get to see her."

"Perhaps you can introduce me to this friend?" laughed Javier, always seeing the lighter side of life.

"You are a lecherous man," laughed Daniel, grateful that his friend was trying to brighten his mood.

The next day, Dianna Hamilton-Gordon knocked on Daniel's apartment door at precisely three o'clock in the afternoon. Her father was waiting outside in his carriage, anxious that the meeting between Dianna and Daniel would be successful. Of course, there was the complication of Catherine, but he was confident that Dianna's news would inspire Catherine to leave Daniel immediately.

Catherine opened the door and to her surprise was confronted with a lovely young woman.

"Good afternoon. Can I help you?" said Catherine.

"Yes, I think you can. I am Dianna Hamilton-Gordon. I am calling on Daniel Leicester. Is he home?"

"Please wait in the hallway," said Catherine formally. "I will fetch him."

Daniel came to the door.

"Dianna," he nodded as frown developed on his face.

"Good day, Daniel."

"Is this a social call?"

"No, Daniel. I have an important matter to discuss with you."

"I wasn't expecting you. I am busy at the moment. Please, leave your calling card," Daniel said abruptly.

"I suggest you see me today, Daniel. This is a matter of urgency, and time is of the essence."

"In that case, please come into my study," he said with reluctance.

Daniel pulled out a chair for Dianna, and she sat down gracefully. She was immaculately dressed. Her auburn hair was in a knot revealing her graceful neck and white skin. Any other man would have been impressed, but Daniel knew that she was a conniving woman who took after her selfish, scheming father.

Catherine was keen to return to her research, but Dianna stopped her.

"You may stay. It is better that you hear this from me—"

"—May I ask, what you want, Dianna?" interrupted Daniel.

Catherine looked at Daniel, but he was oblivious to her gaze. He was searching Diana's face for clues. He was sure that he detected a hint of a small smile at the corners of her mouth. *What is she up to?*

"I am with child. You are the father."

The words were like a hammer blow. Instantly, he felt winded. He looked at Catherine, but she was now staring at Dianna.

"Of course, this will change our lives," cooed Diana, like she was consoling someone at a funeral.

"Obviously, we will have to form a union," she said smoothly, turning her head and looking at Catherine. "We need to inform our parents and calculate when to put it into the social columns. I suggest sooner rather than later before the bairn begins to show."

"I told you that I would never marry you, Dianna."

"You were the first man in my life. You took my—" Dianna's voice trailed off as a wounded expression formed on her face.

Daniel did not know what to say in response to the bare-faced lie. The last thing he wanted was debating Dianna's virtue in front of Catherine, who was now watching the disaster unfold before her eyes with horror. She was determined not to give Dianna the satisfaction of watching her run from the room, even though every fibre in her body wanted to flee.

"I will see you to the door, Dianna," Daniel said calmly.

"I will not have you ruin my reputation," Dianna said. "I will not have you destroy my family's reputation like you have done to Sebastian Pimbleby."

Catherine clenched her jaw to suppress the urge to retaliate.

"Catherine has a husband. You are making a fool of yourself. However, when you marry me, everyone will forget the dreadful scandal that the two of you have caused," Dianna said smugly.

Daniel appeared to be in control of his emotions, but it was merely discipline that kept him from getting up and throttling her.

"Get out of my house and never come back here," the professor bellowed.

He stood up and frogmarched her to the front door. He deposited her at the top of the apartment steps and closed the door without saying goodbye.

Daniel stood with his hands in his pockets and looked out of the window. He watched the coachman assist Dianna into the cab, and he got a glimpse of Sir Rufus as the door closed. *They are as thick as thieves.* Daniel even wondered if the old man and his daughter's greed had made them consider an incestuous relationship to trap him. The last thing he saw was the Hamilton-Gordon coat of arms as the carriage slipped around the corner.

Catherine was devastated, she did not want to see or speak to Daniel. It took several hours for her to calm down. She tried to make sense of what had happened, but there wasn't much to explain. Daniel had bedded the young girl, and she was pregnant. She barely looked eighteen. For Catherine, it was a sickening betrayal.

"Catherine, please come out."

She had waited so long for the man she truly loved. Now everything they had planned together was ripped away from her. *No doubt, the two fathers would compel Daniel to marry Dianna. He doesn't seem the sort of man to let his child grow up without a strong father figure in its life. Even if I were prepared to be his mistress, I would always come second to Dianna. I would be excluded from spending any festivity or celebration with him.* When she imagined Daniel in bed with Dianna, she felt physical pain in her heart. Daniel was her man, her territory and his hands touching that horrible woman made her so angry that she wanted to hurt him as much as he had just hurt her.

She opened the door and stared at him, blankly. Daniel tried to reach out and take her into his arms, but she sidestepped him and walked to the study.

"Is the child yours?"

"Honestly—I don't know," he replied.

"That means something must have happened between you."

Catherine shook her head and tears ran down her face.

"When? Tell me."

"The weekend of Elizabeth birthday's party, just before you got here as the housekeeper," Daniel confessed.

"She is a still child!" Catherine yelled in disgust.

"No, she is not. She is twenty-one."

"She was a virgin."

"No, she wasn't. She was highly experienced."

"How dare you lie to me and expect me to believe that!"

"I know women—and there was nothing innocent about her."

Catherine felt repulsed.

"What are you going to do, Daniel?"

"I don't know yet. But I am not going to marry her. Her father has put me under pressure since that weekend. The two of them have planned this. I smell a rat," Daniel said without emotion.

"The only rat is you, Daniel. How dare you refuse to take responsibility. You are like every other rich man in this city. You use women and cast them aside when you tire of them."

"Rufus Hamilton-Gordon and my father are setting up a company. If I marry Dianna, the joint fortune will be safe in the family forever.

They see it as an insurance policy. For them, forming a marriage contract. Blood ties are far more watertight than relying on a mere business contract."

"If you didn't want to marry her, why was she in your bed?"

Daniel couldn't answer the question. He could say 'simply because he is a man and it was offered on a plate,' but he dared not give Catherine that answer. She looked murderous enough already.

"How can I believe a word you say anymore, Daniel?"

"Because I saw John Cowie, my barrister yesterday, and I have waived my inheritance. There is no point in them forming the alliance. I am sure we will soon find out Dianna's supposed pregnancy is nothing more than a ruse to trap me. Time will prove me right if you'll permit me that chance?"

He walked toward her. She had never seen him that sombre. He put out his arms and hoped she might be drawn to them. Despite all the odds, he was in luck, and she took a few tentative paces towards him. He tried to stroke her hair, but she pulled away.

"I love you, Catherine," he told her. "I will love you for the rest of my life and far beyond."

"It's too late for that. I vowed after my experience with Sebastian that I would never let a man disrespect me again. I don't need to tell you getting another woman pregnant and still professing your love for me counts as disrespect."

She went into the bedroom and began packing a few essentials in her suitcase.

"Where are you going? Please don't leave."

"I will survive without you. I don't need anyone."

"I am begging you not to leave, Catherine. Please listen to me," he said, blocking her path to the door.

"Get out of my way," she snapped.

"I won't let you go. Not like this."

Catherine slapped him across the cheek with such force it left a stinging red mark.

"Get out of my way and don't ever come near me again."

Catherine slammed the door behind her as she left. Her heart was shattered. Looking dishevelled, tears were streaming down her face. She had no idea where she was going. *Anywhere is better than being stuck in there with him!*

17

DOUGIE SIMPSON'S HENCHMEN

Dougie Simpson's two thugs stood outside the apartment, frustrated. Daniel Leicester had not left the building as per his usual routine. There had been no sign of Catherine whatsoever since their vigil began. They were at loggerheads at what to do next.

"This a bloody mess, innit," lamented Tommy the Blade, who had earned the name for his proficiency with a stolen butcher's knife.

"Tis a fekking dangerous job, Tom. Can be a hanging offence if we 'urt her in the struggle," warned his accomplice, Stevie Smith.

"Do yer think ye can handle the man alone?" asked Tommy.

"Not a bleedin' chance! Have ye seen the size of that geezer? And if I knife him, we are as good as dead. This isn't some drunken toff who wandered into the wrong bit of the Old Nichol by mistake. Everyone knows this Leicester fella. The Old Bill will want to catch somebody if he comes to a sticky end. We've been lurking around here for days now. It doesn't take a genius to work out how that might end for us if someone squeals."

"Yeah, Stevie. And the boss won't be best pleased if we botch this," added Tommy. "Dougie would sort out something far worse than the coppers nabbing us."

"All this aggro just for a woman. That husband of hers is mad."

"Just remember this is good money fer us," said Tommy. "And we won't get a penny of it until we get her!"

"It's suicide mission if that professor sort sees us," said Stevie. "I dunno Tom, I say we walk and try again tomorrow."

"Dougie will want us on another job soon. We can't keep sitting here like a pair of lemons."

Catherine hurtled down the stairs to the servants' entrance. She collided with Mr Farley on the way down who greeted her in his usual jolly manner, but she pushed her way past him, her case swinging wildly. He was surprised at her behaviour and wondered why she looked so distraught. Tommy the Blade couldn't believe his eyes when Catherine came tearing out along the path.

"Jesus, Mary and Joseph!" he cursed, "Will yer look at that, Stevie! Straight into our hands, like she's been sent by God himself."

Catherine reached the gate. She saw the two men loitering in the road but took no notice of them. Her only concern was to get as far away from Daniel Leicester as possible. Just as she passed Stevie, he grabbed her by the arm.

"Not a word, my pretty. Do you hear me? Or I cut yer throat."

Daniel flew after Catherine, passing the bewildered Mr Farley who pushed himself up against the wall, afraid of being crushed by the big man, thundering down the stairs like a bowling ball.

He got to the servants' entrance and burst into the courtyard. At the end of the path, he could just see Catherine wrestling with her captors.

By now Catherine was in no mood for any more nonsense, no matter what the risk.

"Who are you?"

"Tommy the Blade," he snarled in a harsh tone.

"Where are you taking me?" she demanded, but they ignored her.

He pushed her up into the cab and threw the luggage in after her, then leapt up to his seat. Stevie was in close pursuit and took the seat next to the driver. The horse received almighty whipping, and the animal tore down the road almost at full gallop.

Tommy shoved his hand over Catherine's mouth, crushing her head against the frame of the cab.

"Any more from you and you are dead," he sneered.

Tommy realised he had said too much. Distracted at the shock of his basic blunder, unconsciously he released his grip a little. Catherine slid her head to one side and began screaming.

"You would have already killed me if you wanted me dead."

"We will leave that up to yer husband, Missy. He's waiting for you at home."

"Let me out now! Let—me—out!" she yelled as she tried to kick open the cab door.

Stevie was getting anxious. *Surely the coppers will hear her making such a racket?*

Tommy, equally concerned, put his hands around her throat.

"I suggest you watch that mouth of yours."

Now gasping for air, Catherine had no choice but to comply.

Back outside his apartment, Daniel was panicking after hearing the words 'Tommy the Blade.'

Now in Kensington, the cab pulled into the courtyard of the Pimbleby mansion. Sebastian rushed out and stood on the steps to see who it was, then began rubbing his hands together with glee.

Tommy escorted Catherine toward him, and Pimbleby grabbed her by her hair. Tommy the Blade gave him one disapproving stare. In a rare display of acquiescence, Sebastian did as he was told, let go of her hair and took her by the arm.

"We want the other half of the money—now!" warned Tommy.

"I will bring it to you in a minute."

"Now, or I'll cut yer throat where ye stand, posh boy."

Sebastian pushed Catherine into the house and dragged her to the parlour where Lady Pimbleby sat waiting expectantly.

Now with his wife back in his possession, Sebastian ignored Tommy and Stevie. They could stand there all night for all he cared. His deal was with Ogilvy and Dougie, not them, and they would be the ones he paid. He slammed the door in their faces.

After fifty minutes of pointless pacing to pass the time, Tommy and Stevie realised that Sebastian had no intention of paying up. It was getting dark. Tiredness and hunger were weakening their resolve. They decided to make their way to Whitechapel, but there were going to be repercussions for Sebastian. Dougie wasn't going to be pleased Pimbleby had reneged on the deal.

For Daniel, reluctant to go to the police in case the men panicked and killed their captive to protect their identities, there was only one man who could help him now.

"Ah, Señor Daniel, come in, come in," Javier smiled.

"Catherine's gone! Two thuggish men pounced on her. They bundled her into a cab. One of them is called Tommy the Blade. Heaven knows what will happen to her."

His rambling woes all tumbled out at once, leaving Javier somewhat baffled by his outburst.

"Stop, Daniel! I can't keep up."

Daniel was finding it difficult to remain calm and kept yammering on. It took some time before Javier could piece together what he meant.

"Tommy the Blade. That sounds like a 'mal nombre.'"

"Yes, whatever that means. Javier. Now, where do I begin?"

"Well, let's begin by finding out Tommy's real name. Then we stand a chance of finding him."

"But who will know?"

"The police."

"Is that wise? What if—"

"Do you have a better suggestion?"

"No," Daniel sighed. "Right then," he said, logic beginning to prevail. "We will walk from here to Spitalfields, and ask every bobby and police station along the way. Somebody must have heard the name. Sounds like a criminal's badge of honour. It's memorable."

"We are going to die in Spitalfields," said Javier.

"Get out of that posh suit, and we stand a better chance of surviving."

The two men embarked on the four-mile walk. They asked every bobby they saw but drew a blank. Eventually, they reached the police station in Spitalfields.

> "I can tell from a mile away you fellas don't belong in these parts, do you? Tommy is a very bad apple," warned the constable. "I suggest you stay away from a chap like him."

Another colleague piped up to reinforce the point.

> "Tommy is one of Dougie Simpson's mobster henchmen. You don't want to go near him. Surely you've read about his antics in the paper? Lads in Dougie's gang are regular visitors to Pentonville. Dougie's a bit too slippery to get involved directly. Hence, he employs men like Tommy."

> "Understood. We must keep clear of Señor Simpson. But where will we find Tommy?" asked Javier undeterred.

> "Sir, do you think I am stupid? Get out of here. Get out of Spitalfields. I am not giving you information that will get yourselves killed. Insane, the pair of you. Whatever gripe you have with Tommy, I suggest you forget about it, while you still can."

Daniel gave a nod of his head to indicate to Javier they should give up on the idea of getting help from the boys in blue. As the men left the station, the two constables looked at each other amazed by the foolhardy attitude they had just witnessed.

"So where to next?" asked Javier.

"Let's look for a pub. There has to be a bartender who knows the gossip."

It took four pubs and four pints before they found a bartender brave enough to assist.

"Tommy spends his leisure time at the Royal Hotel. It's not far from here—third road on the left. Oh, and lads—be careful."

Daniel thanked the man and gave him a generous tip. The barman hoped the next time he saw Daniel's face, it would not be accompanying a murder story in the paper.

Dougie Simpson was not a happy man.

"I didn't think I could hate Pimbleby any more than I did to begin with. Seems I was mistaken. Why didn't you break the bleedin' door down?" demanded Dougie.

"Sir, it's Kensington. Boss, they have coppers everywhere to protect 'em rich nobs."

"He made you idiots wait for an hour—for nothing?"

"Yes, sir," said Stevie. "He said the deal was with you and Ogilvy. We need to get him in a dark alley, boss. Remind him what he agreed to."

"Exactly. You two go back tomorrow. Persuade him a little. Break a couple of fingers or something. You have my permission. You can break an arm if he don't cough up right there and then. Bleedin' weasel."

The Royal Hotel was well lit and looked like a decent establishment from the outside. The windows onto the street were clean. The brass door handles were polished, and a well-dressed concierge stood at the door. Dougie Simpson had done up the place a little, intending to end his evenings in semi-respectable surroundings. The concierge recognised that the two men who ambled inside were not regulars and whispered to the bellboy to alert Tommy. *As long as they spend a bit of money over the bar and then go home, there would be no problems for them. If not, things might not end so well.*

Daniel sat down on a shabby chair that had once been upholstered in pristine fabric. Now, the padded seat was threadbare, and the arms were dirty. He and Javier ordered a whisky to settle their nerves. Daniel wasn't an easily scared man, he had been in dangerous situations before on his travels overseas, but now he felt out of his depth. This wasn't like a barroom brawl with some rowdy sailors. Tommy was a vicious kidnapper, and probably much worse too if the constables were to be believed.

Locals would have known better than to step up to the barman and ask to see Dougie Simpson. For these two fish out of water, it was baffling—and worrying.

"You sure you have the right name?"

"Yes, sir. Quite certain."

Daniel noticed the barman wink at somebody behind him. Moments later, Tommy the Blade sidled up from behind the chair.

From his tall stature, Tommy sussed the man's identity. *How the hell has he tracked me down at this time of night?* Knowing Daniel was bound to be livid, Tommy looked at the big man and felt anxious. *Dougie isn't going to like this.*

"Try anything, or you will get a blade between yer ribs. Ye got that, mate?"

"I'm looking for your boss," Daniel said quietly. "No trouble. Just information."

"Dunno if he'll see yer. He's a busy man, Dougie," replied Tommy.

"Tell him Daniel Leicester is here. I am looking for Catherine Pimbleby, and I have cash."

"Cash you say? Perhaps Dougie might be available after all."

Tommy the Blade took Daniel to the third floor up some creaking stairs, the dark-coloured carpet worn down to the creamy hessian backing in places. Javier stayed in the lounge under instructions to run like hell if things got out of hand.

Dougie Simpson looked at the tall, well-built man. From Daniel's attempt to blend in with his clothing, Dougie knew that he was not dealing with a 'Sebastian Pimbleby' sort. This fellow was a little wilier in his approach with much more of a grasp of the common man.

"Mr Simpson, I am Daniel Leicester."

"Please, take a seat," Dougie said as he reclined in his chair. "What can I do for you?"

Daniel was straight to the point, which impressed Dougie even more.

"I want to find Catherine Pimbleby."

"Nope. Never heard of her."

"What if I told you I know Tommy kidnapped her from my apartment in Mayfair today?" Daniel said to him quietly.

"How would you know that?"

"I heard him introduce himself to Catherine before he bundled her into a cab against her will."

The two men sat in silence for a while.

"This puts me in a very awkward position, Daniel. You see if I tell you where she is, I jeopardise being paid by my other client. He is keen for her to be with him."

"I will pay you double."

Daniel had now captured Dougie's full attention.

"How are you going to pay? Half now and half on delivery?"

"No."

"No?"

"Cash on the hip tomorrow if you give me the address. I will fetch her myself. Do we have a deal?"

Dougie pondered the offer. He could see that the man was serious, and he was confident that Daniel was good for the money.

"Two thousand pounds says yes."

"When?"

"I can pay you first thing in the morning."

"How do I know it's not a trap?" asked Dougie.

"Because I love her."

Dougie was impressed with the man's candour.

"Do you want us to soften her a little, persuade her to behave?" asked Dougie.

"What do you mean?"

"Well, you know, my men can always—" He didn't finish the sentence.

Daniel walked toward him, his face now inches away from Dougie's.

"If you touch a hair on her head, there will be hell to pay. Now, do we have an agreement?"

Dougie smiled. Daniel had passed the test.

"Yes, Professor Leicester. We do."

Lady Pimbleby had instructed Sebastian not to lay a hand on Catherine, but the temptation to push her about was too great. He shoved her into a tiny bedroom, and she went sprawling across the floor.

"One murmur from you, Catherine, and you will get the beating of your life."

He closed the door and locked it. It was not the worst that she had suffered by his hand, but she was anxious for what was to come. The house was very still, and she had seen no servants which troubled her. Sebastian clearly wanted privacy.

Catherine couldn't sleep, and by morning she was exhausted. She heard the key turn in the door. It swung open, and Sebastian swooped in behind it.

"Mother is in the breakfast room. She wants to see you."

"Your mother? Here?"

Sebastian grabbed his wife roughly and pushed her towards the staircase.

The day was dull and grey, and the breakfast room looked bleak. She decided there must be some servants in the house because she saw some food on the server.

Her mother-in-law sat at the window and looked out at the street as the people began to stir.

"Catherine, my dear," greeted Lady Pimbleby, taking in her daughter-in-law's dishevelled appearance.

She sat down opposite her and looked at the cunning old woman.

"I don't want to be here," complained Catherine.

"You are married to my son. You belong by his side."

"Your son is a monster. I told you that many years ago, but you wouldn't help me," Catherine protested, emboldened by long-suppressed anger.

"You are an embarrassment, Catherine. If you had just stayed at home and been more accommodating, we wouldn't be in this mess. You fled from your marriage. You are having a torrid public affair with another man. You are a disgrace. Sebastian should have dealt with you years ago."

Lady Pimbleby's voice was bitter and lacked an ounce of compassion. She glared at Catherine over a hooked, beak-like nose, her blue eyes narrowing. *She looks more like a witch than a woman.*

"You and your son only wanted my family's money. That is why Sebastian forced himself upon me and then blackmailed me into marrying him."

"Maybe so, my dear, but it did not mean that you had the right to make yourself the laughing stock of London, and drag the Pimblebys down with you."

"I am leaving, and you will not stop me," Catherine announced, confident she could overpower the old woman. She stood up and began walking towards the door.

"Sebastian, come here, please."

Listening in by the doorway, her son took his cue.

"I agree with you, Sebastian. You have tolerated Catherine's wayward behaviour far too long. Do what you need to do to get her under control."

Sebastian followed his wife into the hallway. As she reached the staircase, he pulled her back.

"Step away," she hissed.

"You will live with me until the day you die, Catherine, or I will lock you away until you are submissive. I will make you change your habits."

He pushed her up the stairs towards the landing. Catherine tried to fight him off, but in his rage, he was too strong. He pushed her into the small room, and this time he followed her in. Catherine turned around and tried to make a run for the door, but it was futile. As if he were back at Eton playing rugby, Sebastian wrestled her to the floor, pinning her down. She could smell his breath and feel his intentions. Grabbing her hair, he planted a rough kiss on her mouth. Desperate to escape, she bit him, and blood streamed from his mouth into hers. It made her gag.

As Sebastian stopped for a moment to investigate his injury, she scrambled to her feet. Her insolence enraged him, and he punched her with his full weight behind him, lifting Catherine off her feet. She went flying backwards, collided with a cupboard and fell unconscious on the floor like a rag doll.

When she came to, it took a moment for her to realise the danger she was in. She pushed herself up and sat against the cupboard. Her face felt smashed, and her nose was bleeding. She crawled to the door and pulled herself up. She anticipated that the door would be locked, but tried the handle anyway. Miraculously, it gave way, and the door opened. The house was silent. Catherine tiptoed down the staircase, too anxious to feel the pain. The front door was tantalisingly close. She almost jumped out of her skin when she heard the jangling doorbell. *No!*

A staff member opened the door, and she heard a voice. *Daniel?*

"I am here to see Sebastian Pimbleby."

Catherine collapsed on the stairs and began to weep. Hearing the thud, Daniel looked up. He pushed the servant to one side and flew up the stairs two at a time. Her head was hidden behind her hands until he gently teased them away. The bruising on her face was clearly apparent.

"He did this to you, didn't he?"

Catherine couldn't answer. Like a small child that had just skinned its knee, all she could do was sob.

Hearing the commotion Sebastian and his mother ran out of the breakfast room.

"What are you doing in my house? Get away from her!" Sebastian screamed.

Daniel put his arm around Catherine and helped her stand up. Her knees quaked, and he had to steady her. Slowly, they descended the stairs as a red-faced irate Lady Pimbleby looked on.

"Sebastian, please tell me you are not going to let that man come into your home and drag your wife out of it?"

Daniel glared at her. She was glaring at Sebastian who had ignored her order.

"Come now, Catherine, don't be scared. I have a cab waiting outside. Please, just this once, let me take control."

When they reached the cab, a smiling man was sitting in it.

"Good day Señora. I am Javier, let me help you. Daniel has told me so much about you, and you are every bit as lovely as he described."

He took her hand and helped her take a seat, then put his coat around her. She pulled it around her tightly, as if she were making a shield.

"Look after her," shouted Daniel.

"Come back," yelled Javier.

"I am not finished yet."

Daniel rushed back into the house.

"How dare you enter my home like this?" Lady Pimbleby shrieked.

"Where is your son?"

"I don't know," lied the old lady.

Daniel turned to the servant. "Where did he go?"

The servant directed his eyes to the stairs.

Daniel rushed to the first landing and started flinging doors open, searching for Sebastian. He found a door that was locked. *So, the pig farming little coward is hiding away, is he—now that he's facing me rather than beating a woman black and blue?*

It was the second time Daniel had to do this, but there would be no third. He kicked at the lock with all his might, and he could hear the wood begin to shatter. It was a solid oak door and took a concerted effort to make it give way.

He stormed into the room and saw Sebastian standing defensively with a marble lamp base in his hand, but Daniel's wrath made him fearless. Sebastian threw the lamp at Daniel but missed. Without saying a word, in an anger-fuelled trance, he grabbed Sebastian by the head and repeatedly hit it against the bedpost until he felt some hands pulling him away.

"Daniel!" Javier shouted. "Daniel, stop it. You are going to kill him."

It took the combined strength of Javier and the servant to pull Daniel off. Lady Pimbleby had finally made it up the stairs and stood in the doorway.

Sebastian, with his head bleeding profusely, was almost unconscious. "My God," she wheezed. "What have you done to him?

Javier stared at her in amazement. *The lovely Catherine is in the coach severely beaten, and this horrible old woman was only concerned about her monster of a son?*

Daniel glared at Lady Pimbleby, stunned by her selfishness.

"Catherine is my son's wife! How dare you intervene like this, Daniel!"

He tried to get to Lady Pimbleby, but Javier pulled his friend out of the room.

> "Come on, Daniel. We must go, Señor. Your work here is done. This horrible business is over."

18

JUST DESSERTS

Dougie sat in his chair and smiled. He had made a significant amount of money from Daniel Leicester. He was impressed that the man was satisfied to face Pimbleby alone. It kept the transaction wonderfully uncomplicated. All he wanted to do was find the woman and keep his nose clean.

As far as Dougie was concerned, he and Daniel were square—the relationship was over. But his eyes blacked with fury when he thought about Sebastian Pimbleby, the man who had seen fit to double-cross him and renege on settling his outstanding debt. Dougie didn't like that.

The Pall Mall Club was bursting with politicians and industrialists. Protection of the Suez region pivoted on the provision of British-made arms and munitions, and everybody in the club was still vying for a piece of the lucrative business. Men stood in little huddles discussing, relegating and resurrecting old friendships in the name of profit.

Sir Rufus Hamilton-Gordon and Sir James Leicester sat at a small table in the far corner of the dining room. Amid the hum of activity and excitement, the two men looked at each other glumly.

"I have summoned him to the manor this weekend," Sir James said.

"Do you think that he will make an appearance?"

"Yes, Daniel seems to thrive on confrontation these days."

"Have you told him that Dianna and I would be in attendance?"

"Of course not! He will behave even worse than I expect him to."

"Yes, I have experienced that fiery side of his character," lamented Sir Rufus.

"He is going to be a father, and I have expectations of him."

"I am glad we agree," said Sir Rufus with an evil smile.

Daniel and Catherine arrived at the Leicester family home in a raging storm. It wasn't only the weather that was tempestuous. When Sir James saw Catherine in tow, he scowled.

"What is she doing with you?"

"I am going to marry her father. I have told you this."

"That's what you think," growled his father.

Daniel could not have cared less. His mother was always more friendly, and she welcomed Catherine as if entirely oblivious to the gossip about her that had circulated London for years.

Elizabeth stormed down the stairs to greet her brother but stopped dead when she saw Catherine.

"Who is this?" demanded Elizabeth without acknowledging her.

"Catherine Frankland," replied Daniel.

Elizabeth looked Catherine up and down with disdain.

"Daniel, you do know that Dianna will be here this weekend?"

"What?"

"Dianna and her father are spending the weekend here. Dianna says there will be an announcement."

"Did she?"

"Yes, and she says it has something to do with you two. They will be here soon."

Catherine looked at Daniel. She was overwhelmed by Elizabeth's rudeness, and she felt close to tears. He steered her to a quiet corner.

"Daniel, I want to leave this place," she whispered, her head bowed down.

Daniel put his arms around her and squeezed her to his chest, "I promise that you will never have to return here, Catherine. This one last visit is all I ask so we can sort this Dianna business once and for all."

"I can't face that woman again, Daniel. She is going to take you away from me."

"Never," Daniel whispered in her ear and then kissed her neck. "I will never let you go. Please, darling, I know in my bones this pregnancy is a scheme drawn up by Sir Rufus. Give me a chance to prove it. That's all I ask."

Daniel watched the Hamilton-Gordon coach turn into the driveway and pull up on the gravel. Sir Rufus's feet crunched on the stones as he got out. He turned to help Dianna tentatively out of the coach as if she were royalty. They were putting on a tremendous display of grandeur. Catherine saw the beautiful young woman glide towards the house, her head held high with an aristocratic bearing. She, however, felt humiliated with her face covered in scars and bruises.

"Don't let them intimidate you, Catherine. It is all an act," Daniel said loudly enough for his parents to hear.

The father and daughter were ushered into the house and led straight to the parlour, aglow with gentle golden lamplight and warming fires to welcome the special guests. Daniel thought back to the first time he had laid eyes on Dianna. She had seemed unsullied, beautiful, innocent. Now, Daniel saw her for what she was, experienced, manipulative and cunning. When he looked at her, he only had regrets.

Everything went as his mother had planned it—warm fires, sweet sherry, high tea—just as society deemed perfect.

"Elizabeth, Catherine, can you please leave the room? We need to speak to Daniel alone," said Sir James.

"You can stay with me, Catherine," said Daniel defiantly.

"Good God, Daniel," shouted his father.

"Don't you dare try and intimidate her. Catherine is with me. I am not letting her leave this room," he retaliated.

Catherine felt like crying, but she kept her composure and sat as quietly as she could, wishing herself away from these horrible people.

"If she can stay, so can I," announced Elizabeth.

"Get out," Daniel roared at her.

Lady Leicester became pale. The genteel afternoon was not proceeding as she had planned it.

"Oh my," said Sir Rufus in bewilderment, "if this is a bad time to broach the subject, we can wait until tomorrow."

"Get on with it, Rufus," Daniel demanded.

"Well, since you know Dianna's condition, it is time that we sought clarity on the arrangement going forward."

"Of course," nodded Lady Leicester. "It is a bit of a surprise. It might have been a mistake announcing it this way, but we understand the severity of the situation. We just cannot afford the news to spread beyond the room," she said and looked at Catherine.

Catherine looked down in fear and humiliation. Sir James looked at his son.

"Now find your backbone, old boy. I think it will be good for Catherine to hear the truth so that she can return to her husband with no false promises from you."

"I agree," said Dianna in an innocent voice, "Catherine, he can't marry you until she is divorced. I am pregnant with his child. And after all the trouble you caused the Pimbleby's, clearly, I am the sensible choice."

The two fathers nodded their heads in agreement.

"Yes," said Sir James, "Let us try and get things back to normal should we? Catherine, my dear, you will not be a part of the family's future."

"I agree with you, father," Daniel said, at the same time secretly squeezing Catherine's hand to reassure her.

"Thank God you have come to your senses, my boy."

The broad grin that suddenly appeared on Sir James' face was to vanish just as rapidly.

"Mr Cowie, my solicitor has drawn up some documents, father. I am waiving my inheritance. I am no longer a part of this family's future, and neither is Catherine."

Dianna and Sir Rufus looked at each other.

"What are you saying?" demanded Dianna.

"It's simple, Dianna. I don't want to inherit the estate. It can be left to my brother, along with the title."

"You can't do this to me," screamed Dianna.

"Daniel, have you lost your mind?" yelled his father. "I thought this legal nonsense was an idle threat. I never expected you to go ahead with it."

Daniel turned around and confronted Sir Rufus.

"Dianna isn't pregnant, is she?" asked Daniel.

The jumpy little man could not meet Daniel's eyes.

"Tell the truth, Sir Rufus, or I will choke it out of you."

Sir Rufus gave a nervous little smile.

"No, she is not,"

"Do you think I will marry you if you have nothing?" shrieked Dianna.

Daniel did not need to hear any more. He took a relieved Catherine by the hand and led her to their waiting cab.

Within a minute, they had disappeared down the end of the Leicesters' long drive.

Sebastian stood on the pier waiting for Ogilvy who was late as usual. It was almost dusk, and the sky was red. The docks were quiet except for the odd stranger on his way home. A man approached from a distance. He was dressed in humble workman's clothes. His cloth hat sat at an angle, and he wore a ragged coat to keep himself warm.

When he got to Sebastian, he fished out a battered cigarette from his pocket then stopped to ask for a light. Sebastian unbuttoned his jacket to remove his box of matches.

In his peripheral vision, Sebastian saw a flash of steel but did not have time to register exactly what was happening. He recognised Tommy the Blade when it was too late. Tommy tugged the jacket to one side to get a clear view of Sebastian's chest. The entire blade plunged through his ribs like a hot knife through butter. Sebastian collapsed, clutching at the wound. Blood seeped through his fingers and began to flow onto the pier. He died within minutes and was found lying in a pool of blood the same deep red colour as the smog-filled sky. Tommy melted away into the shadows.

Daniel and Catherine honeymooned on the picturesque island of Capri and swam naked in the clear water of the Blue Grotto.

Back on shore, Catherine sat astride the body of her husband. He lay beneath her like a god from the Roman legends. The sun had baked down upon their bodies, and his muscular arms were enhanced by a bronzed tan. He had one strong hand on each of her hips and was carefully guiding her. Her long curly hair cascaded down her back, and he became more aroused as he watched her move.

His gaze travelled upwards to her grey eyes, and she smiled at him, her sensual mouth expressing the pleasure that she felt.

Daniel was experienced. Over the years, he had many women to compare her with but he knew that for as long as he lived, she was the most beautiful woman that he would ever make love to.

Printed in Great Britain
by Amazon